# MARKED DECK AT TOPANGO WELLS

Center Point
Large Print

Also by William Colt MacDonald and available from Center Point Large Print:

*Peaceful Jenkins*
*Mascarada Pass*
*Showdown Trail*
*Guns Between Suns*
*Law and Order, Unlimited*
*The Gun Branders*

# MARKED DECK AT TOPANGO WELLS

## William Colt MacDonald

Center Point Large Print
Thorndike, Maine

This Center Point Large Print edition
is published in the year 2025 by arrangement with
Golden West Inc.



The text of this Large Print edition is unabridged.
In other aspects, this book may vary
from the original edition.
Printed in the United States of America
on permanent paper sourced using
environmentally responsible foresting methods.
Set in 16-point Times New Roman type.

ISBN: 979-8-89164-489-2

The Library of Congress has cataloged this record
under Library of Congress Control Number: 2024949808

# I

The strong wind that had lifted in the early afternoon across the semi-desert country to the east of Topango Wells, by three o'clock had risen to gale-like violence, filling the atmosphere with dust and sand and tiny gritty particles, sharply stinging faces and nostrils of man and beast with a punishing ferocity—when they were exposed while still abroad. There weren't many of those.

Such wind-storms happened infrequently, but residents of Topango recognized the signs—they called them Topango Howlers—and made haste to get their beasts under shelter, hastily put up shutters, when such existed, weight down such objects as might be carried away, batten doors and windows with rags stuffed into cracks, and then withdraw to the safety of indoors.

Topango wasn't much of a town. Just a single street, dusty in summer and muddy when the rains came, lined on either side with a row of hitch-racks, behind which rose a series of false-fronted buildings, two or three being actually of two-story construction. Strange to say, for a cowtown in the Southwest, there was but a single saloon, known as the Topango, owned and operated by one Hippodrome Casey, an individual of immense proportions, usually known as Hippo.

There was a single general store, a barber shop, which was on the verge of bankruptcy, one restaurant operated by a Chinese, a pool hall and Mexican chili-and-enchilada shop, and where it was said, if you were known, a drink of *tequila* could be had from under the counter.

Topango was also the end of the T.N. & A.S. railroad line, with a depot on a raised dirt platform, a small freight shed and some cattle pens at the east end of town. For the rest there was a scattering of houses, both frame and adobe. A few cottonwoods grew here and there. There were the usual dogs, cats and chickens pecking in the street on normal days.

The wind howled relentlessly. The air was a thick sandy dusty hue. By three o'clock the sun was almost obscured. By five it looked like a thin silver dollar suspended in space. By six o'clock it had disappeared altogether. Shutters and doors banged, trash was hurled helter-skelter along the street or was lifted on the sandy haze to flutter like a wounded buzzard. A few loose tin cans rattled and banged along the way. And always there was the relentless howling of the gale.

The point is that the wind-storm was bringing a quality that was to surpass even the violence of the storm, though no one as yet suspected it.

Before three o'clock such cowhands as were in Topango, recognizing the signs, had tightened cinches, climbed into saddles and beat a retreat for the home ranch to the west, where good grazing country prevailed, taking any one of the trails fanning out from the town.

Remained only Kelt Flecker, foreman of the Circle-F, and three of his men, who stood morosely at Hippodrome Casey's bar with bottles and glasses before them. Hippodrome had long since put up his shutters, and the saloon would have been shrouded in darkness, except for the lighted oil lamps suspended from the ceiling here and there. Shining glasses were reflected in the back-bar mirror. On the walls were tacked a few pictures from a pink-sheeted periodical, depicting burlesque actresses, prizefighters and racehorses. Three bare wood tables, scarred with scratches and rings from liquor bottles and glasses, were accompanied by straight-backed chairs.

Hippodrome was not only fat, he was very fat, ponderous, somewhere in the neighborhood of three-hundred pounds, though he wasn't very tall. His jowls hung in fleshly flaps on his neck. His hair was sparse. The apron tied about his waist looked as though it might have been designed for a beer barrel. But he kept a clean saloon; nobody denied that.

Kelt Flecker was a somewhat bulky-constructed man, wide of shoulder, with small shrewd eyes. He wore corduroys, riding boots and a flimsy vest over his woolen shirt. His weather-beaten sombrero was pushed to the back of his head and a scarred holster, holding a forty-five caliber Colt hung low at his right hip.

Of the three hands with him, there was Tim Beadle, tall and lantern-jawed; George Corwin, a hard-bitten individual with a broken nose that had been poorly set; and Herb Jacklin, a bullet-headed man with a sort of rat-trap mouth which seemed only a straight line in his weathered features. All three men wore range togs and all toted forty-five six-shooters, which appeared to be the only objects in full commission. Certainly, their clothing appeared much the worse for wear.

"Better set 'em up again, Hippo," Flecker growled. "I wonder if this goddamn Howler is ever going to let up."

Hippodrome placed bottles and fresh glasses on the bar, and retrieved the silver dollar Flecker slid toward him.

"Should peter out come deep night," Hippo observed, making change with thick stubby fingers. "You fellers should have started back when it started to blow. Didn't you realize—?"

Flecker swore. "Certain we knew what to expect. But I had to ride in to see Bristol Capron. He kept me too long with his damn talking. I damn nigh told him to shut his trap once—"

Hippodrome snickered. "But being he is manager of the Randall Land and Cattle Company, you didn't dare, eh, Kelt?"

Flecker shot an angry look at the fat barkeep.

Finally, he snarled, "Give me credit for knowin' which side my bread is buttered on, Hippo."

Hippodrome grinned. "So now you've buttered your bread and you can lie in it."

"Someday, Hippo," Flecker growled, "you're going to catch your comeuppance, trying to be funny. Your mind, like your carcass, is too fat for such capers—"

What Hippodrome might have retorted was interrupted by an explosive opening of the front door of the saloon as a tall, lean individual covered with a sort of dusty-gray shroud forced his way into the interior of the saloon. If it'd been white, so thick was the dust, he might have been mistaken for a ghost. With something of an effort he turned and forced his weight against the door in an attempt to reclose it, despite the wind endeavoring to resist his strength. Finally with a prodigious amount of exertion the door was made to close once again.

The men at the bar eyed the fellow's struggles with interest, though no one offered to assist. They were making out now, beneath the shrouding of dust, a man in cowpuncher togs, Colt slung at his hip and carrying a Winchester rifle. Other details came into view: the man wore a short coat; a bandanna was tied across his face, covering all but his eyes; a second bandanna crossed his sombrero and was tied under his chin, thus keeping the hat in place.

No one had said anything so far. The newcomer first lowered the bandanna from his face and the men at the bar now saw he was young—probably under thirty. Next he untied the second bandanna from his sombrero, shook the dust from it and removed the hat. Now, Hippodrome and the others saw that the man was a redhead—flaming brick-colored red. Neither did he speak. Apparently he was paying no attention to those at the bar.

Removing the sombrero was a preliminary to using it to slap the gathered dust from his clothing—coat, Levi's, boots underwent a thorough brushing-off. Clouds of dust lifted from his exertions; a thin haze lifted in the barroom, under the vigorous slapping of clothing. High-heeled riding boots, somewhat run-down at heels, got a careful wiping.

Hippodrome Casey, eyeing the dust emanating from the stranger, observed rather caustically, "Y'know you might just as well have left the door open, so long as you figure to bring the outdoors in."

"Damn nigh did," the man replied with a short laugh, "only I was afraid that little breeze might suck me into the street again." He went on with his cleaning-up motions.

"Huh! Little breeze? Breeze?" George Corwin blurted.

The stranger didn't answer that, but continued

his cleaning job. He shook out one bandanna and carefully wiped off his rifle; next his six-shooter came in for an inspection and was carefully dusted before being replaced in the scarred holster. Now, carrying the rifle, he made his way to the bar, spur rowels jangling across the floor.

Hippodrome smiled. "Feeling cleaner, cowboy?"

"Some," the stranger admitted, "though a mite of lubrication might ease the grit out of my joints and carcass."

Casey set out a glass of water. It disappeared at a gulp. Casey set out a second glass, which was consumed more slowly. Casey asked, "That bring some relief, stranger?"

"It helped a heap—anyway, it moistened the mud in my mouth. Now if you only had a cold beer." He waited.

"Not ice-cold but some chilled. We don't see ice very often in Topango." Hippodrome turned ponderously from his bar and reached to a small cupboard space beneath the bar mirror, before which hung a wide length of wet burlap, and came up, grunting, with a bottle of beer, which was placed on the bar together with a glass. With a screwdriver he lifted out the small metal stopper in the mouth of the bottle, and poured the glass half-full.

The stranger eyed the foamy liquid with pleasure, but before lifting it, he said to Hippodrome,

“Could be your other customers would care to join me.”

Hippodrome waddled along the bar. “The gent’s buying. What’s your pleasure?”

So far, with the exception of Corwin’s brief comment, none of them had said anything, but all eyed sharply every move the newcomer made. Now they gave orders, Flecker taking a cigar, the other three Old Crow whisky. They nodded brief thanks.

The stranger seemed to lose his nose in the beer, then set it down with a long sigh of satisfaction. Flecker lighted his cigar and then made his way to the newcomer’s side.

Flecker hinted, “I always like to know a man’s name when I’m beholden to him for buying. I’m Kelt Flecker. Rod of the Circle-F.”

“Knight’s my name—Jerry Knight. Glad to know you, Flecker.”

“Ridin’ far, Knight?” Flecker asked as the two shook hands.

“Not right off.” Knight grinned.

“I mean when this Howler passes.”

“Could be. Then again, maybe not,” Knight said quietly. He wasn’t quite certain he liked Flecker’s probing. He went on, “You said you liked to have the name when a man buys for you. I like to know who I’m buying for.”

“Oh, yeah, sure.” Flecker gestured down the bar. “Three of my top hands—Tim Beadle,

George Corwin and Herb Jacklin. Boys, meet Knight—Jerry Knight he said his name is. Our barkeep here is Hippodrome Casey, the biggest man this side of Barnum's Jumbo, the elephant."

Hippodrome reached across the bar and shook hands. The other three men gave brief nods and turned back to their drinks.

They were, Knight was thinking, not a particularly social bunch. He poured the rest of his beer into the glass.

Flecker exhaled another puff of cigar smoke. "You were saying, Knight, that maybe you'd ride on and maybe not. Weren't figuring on staying in Topango, were you?"

"That depends."

"On what?"

"On whether I can tie on with some outfit hereabouts."

"You mean punching?"

"Right. It's the only trade I got—prodding cow-critters."

"Where you been doing your riding?"

Knight gave the brands of various outfits.

Flecker scowled. "Never heard of any of 'em."

"They're all well east of here."

"Seems to me a feller of your age, if he's worked for so many spreads, must be something of a boomer—or maybe not worth his salary."

"Never had any trouble," the redhead stated mildly.

"Confess up to it then," Flecker said shortly. "You're what I call a saddle-tramp—just riding grub-line and taking a job now and then."

Knight laughed somewhat sheepishly. "Could be you've hit the nail on the head. To tell the truth I like to see new range, but I'd be glad to stick around here for a spell if I could get on with some spread."

Flecker gave a dubious shake of the head. "The Circle-F—I run things there—ain't doing any hiring. I doubt anybody else is, either. Fact is, there ain't too many spreads hereabouts, since them fool hoe-men took over—"

"Hoe-men?" Knight asked.

Flecker explained. "You know, them hayseeds from the east. Come out here and figure they can dry-farm, raise corn and 'taters and beans and such. A few chickens. They don't get far in this range. Good grazing country for beef, but out on them flats to the south, water is damn scarce. Some can't raise enough to hardly feed theirselves. A good many were smart enough to know when they were licked, and pulled out pronto. Any fool should know 't'ain't farmin' country in that region."

Knight nodded he understood. "And all their hoeing won't bring enough moisture up, eh?"

"Nor their spading and plowing, nuther. A few has some scrawny hosses they brung in. Some of the critters already died. Why, a coupla times I've seen some of them idiots with their wife and kids hitched to the plow. Stubborn fools!" Flecker swore disgustedly. "This here is cow-country, and anybody tries to use it for anything else is bound to run into a peck of trouble."

"That so?" Knight seemed interested. "What sort of trouble you mean?"

"What do you think I mean, Knight?" Flecker sneered. "If you get a burr under your bronc's saddle, what do you do?"

"Get rid of the burr," Knight replied promptly.

Flecker gave a nasty laugh. "You get the idea, fellow." He changed the subject. "No, I can't use another hand, and I don't figure any of the others can either. 'Course, come beef-roundup, you might get a chance to get on a payroll for a short spell."

"Reckon I'll just have to stick around until fall roundup starts then," Knight said soberly.

"You could try that"—Flecker shrugged—"providing you got enough cash to see you through the next couple months."

"I got enough dinero to make out, I reckon," Knight admitted.

"How much?" Flecker asked, showing a new interest.

Knight smiled. "Enough," he returned non-committally.

Flecker seemed to lose interest. "Damnit," he growled, consulting a watch from a fob pocket, "it's after six o'clock. I'm hungry. My gut is beginning to think my throat has been slit. But I ain't goin' to go out in this Howler." He nodded. "See you again, maybe," and sauntered back to rejoin his men.

The four stood talking in low tones a few minutes, while Jerry Knight carried on a desultory conversation with Hippodrome Casey. Casey asked, "Your hoss out front, Knight?"

Knight shook his red head. "I left him in your shelter out back after he'd damn near drunk your water tank empty. Gave him a sort of brushing-down with the saddle blanket. Better protection back there."

Hippodrome nodded. "You should have come in the back door."

"I tried, but it was locked."

"Oh, yeah. I forgot that. But you have to keep things pretty tight when these Howlers come—"

A strong blast of wind rattled cans, street signs and shutters along the way. Gritty sand was sifting in beneath the front doors again.

Flecker called from down the bar. "Hey, Knight, we're going to draw cards to see who goes down to the Chinaman's restaurant and brings back some sandwiches. Want to get in?"

Knight shook his head. "Leave me out, thanks."

The bullet-headed Herb Jacklin uttered a caustic laugh. "Afeared you might lose, cowpoke?"

Knight smiled. "Exactly that, Jacklin. I'd just

as soon starve as buck that gale again so soon."

"Tell you what, gents," Hippodrome put in. "I got part of a ham here, cold, and some crackers and pickles and cookies. Sort of like to keep a snack on hand, case'n a feller gets hungry—"

"For God's sakes," Flecker bellowed, "whyn't you say so before? I'm starved fit to eat my boot-taps. Set the mess out."

Hippodrome put some tin plates on his bar, including one for himself. Then from the cupboard where he kept his bottled beer he drew out a large section of ham on a platter. A jar of pickles was produced, crackers and cookies, a triangular chunk of "rat-trap" cheese. With a sharp knife, Hippodrome started to slice the ham and cheese. The men helped themselves and ate hungrily in silence for the next ten minutes. By the time they'd concluded, with sighs of satisfaction, ham and cheese had about disappeared. No one said anything about paying for the grub, until Jerry Knight proposed, "So long as I was the one that spoiled that card-drawing idea to see who'd go to the Chinaman's restaurant, I reckon I ought to stand for this. It's on me, gents."

He dropped a couple of silver dollars on the bar, then produced from another pocket a small roll of bills, from which he peeled a ten to place on the bar.

Hippodrome shoved back the bill. "The coins will cover it, Redhead," he stated. "Thanks."

Flecker raised his voice: “So long as these other bustards ain’t got the decency to say much-obliged for the feed, Knight, I’m saying it for ’em. Y’know, I might get to like a man of your caliber.”

“Thanks. Y’mean you’ll put me on your pay-roll?” Jerry laughed.

Flecker said warily, “I didn’t say that. Before any hand swings a rope under me, I want to know what sort of mind he has. Can he take it when the chips are down?”

“Know any way to prove me?” Knight asked gravely.

“We-ell, so long as we ’pear to be stuck here until the wind goes down, I was about to suggest a few hands of poker. Now, I always say that nothing brings out a man’s behavior under pressure like a good tough poker game.” He turned to his hands, “What do you say, boys?”

“Suits us,” from the other three.

Pretending to mop off his bar with a damp rag, Hippodrome leaned close to Knight, whispering, “Don’t have nothing to do with it. Kelt saw your roll.”

Jerry whispered back, “Maybe I intended he should.” Then raised his voice, “Fine idea, Flecker. I don’t seem to have much else to do.”

“Spoken like a true cowpoke.” Flecker nodded with a wide grin. “Hippo, let’s have a new deck—seal unbroken, d’you hear?”

Hippodrome tossed a fresh deck on the bar. Flecker moved it along the bar to Knight. “Here, Redhead, break the seal on that package and we can get started.”

Somewhere on the street a shutter squeaked and then started to bang noisily in the gale. A door slammed and through the howling of the gale they caught the sudden frantic cursing in a man’s voice. There came an abrupt loud clatter, and the cursing changed to piercing wails of pain.

Flecker guffawed. “Somebody’s shutter came off and hit the galoot on the head, I’m betting. Here’s hoping he got a fractured noggin.” His men joined in the laughter.

Knight said, “We were going to play a few hands of poker, remember? Let’s get started.”

They made their way across the room to a bare table and arranged five straight-backed chairs. There was no talk as to who should deal first. Flecker simply took the cards, riffled them a few times and then commenced to deal around.

Overhead, a thin dusty haze swam in the vicinity of the suspended oil lamp.

# II

The game had been going a couple of hours now. Now and then Hippodrome was called to fetch drinks or cigars, then retired to a stool behind his bar to catch catnaps. Tobacco smoke hung in a wave above the players, to be dispersed now and then when a stronger gust than usual forced its way through shutters and under doors.

Knight had been nursing two bottles of beer during the game, while the others ran to stronger drinks. Now and then Hippodrome awakened for a few moments to gravely eye the players and sadly shake his head when he saw Knight losing.

Once, Hippodrome announced, "Sounds like the wind has died down quite a bit."

Nobody seemed to hear him. He resumed his nap.

At first, Knight had won a few small pots, but when the big ones came up, he never seemed to hold the right cards. His roll of bills had slimmed down considerably.

But still the game went on, hour after hour, with Knight clinging doggedly to certain hopes, hopes he knew in his mind were certain to be frustrated.

Hippodrome Casey roused again. "Hey, you cow-nurses, do . . ."

If anyone heard him there was no response. The deal went round from man to man. Once Flecker commiserated, “Cards don’t seem to be running your way, Redhead.”

Knight smiled. “Luck’s bound to change, Flecker.”

“Hope so,” Flecker stated sympathetically. “I always hate to see it poured on a stranger, even when I’m lucky.”

“Thanks for your kind hopes,” Knight said drolly. “I had almost commenced to feel like that verse in the Bible that says, ‘A certain man went down from Jerusalem to Jericho and . . .’ ” Knight paused. “I forget how the rest goes. Maybe something about a stranger. I dunno.”

“You a churchgoer, Knight?” Flecker asked.

“Now and then—”

George Corwin interrupted, “Say, I heard that Bible saying somewhere. It goes on something about how this hombre fell among thieves.” His voice lifted angrily: “You hintin’ we’re thieves?”

Knight laughed softly. “No, I wasn’t hinting. It was your words, not mine.”

Corwin glared at Knight. Knight smiled, but it was only a smile of the lips. Now Corwin was realizing how cold Knight’s steel-gray eyes could be. Corwin wondered if in some way he had been challenged. A look of confusion entered his features.

“So don’t jump to any conclusions, Corwin,”

Knight was advising quietly. "Let's get going. It's your deal."

"But—" Corwin found his voice.

"Shut up, George, and deal the cards," Flecker ordered crisply.

Play continued. Through the wide cracks of shutters outside the saloon windows, a faint dawn breeze seemed to filter, not enough to even rattle the windowpanes any more. It affected the waves of smoke above the players' heads, lifting it in gentle swirls and helping to make a trifle brighter the illumination spread by the shaded oil lamp overhead.

After a time, Hippodrome went out the back door and if the players had been listening they'd have heard him removing his shutters from the windows. Now, the low-burning wick in the oil lamp was forced to compete palely with the faint gray morning light entering the windows.

Hippodrome returned, announcing that daylight had come, and it was time to quit and fork horses for home.

Flecker half-snarled, "Let be, Hippo. Knight deserves a chance to win back his money. Don't bother us."

Cards were dealt from time to time, with the players' hands moving restlessly above scattered heaps of money, or picking up and discarding cards. No one spoke to any extent now.

Gray dawn spread swiftly along the silent

deserted street of Topango Wells. Along the eastern horizon there came a softness of rose-pink which blended with the mauve of early morning. Down the street a way, a dog howled when its early-rising owner caught it eating some spilled garbage in the roadway and gave it an angry kick.

"Hey," Tim Beadle announced as Flecker raked in another pot, "it's day."

"But Knight's deal," Jacklin put in, chuckling at the feeble joke. "All Knight play, you might say." The cards went around again, Jerry Knight's face a calm mask, revealing nothing to the others. They picked up their hands, Knight studying his cards intently.

Flecker moved impatiently. "Well, how you making it, Knight?"

"Not so well," Knight admitted, now smiling rather whimsically.

Betting commenced, and was raised from time to time. George Corwin had dropped out. Still Jerry studied his cards while the others waited.

Finally he shoved two dollars to the center of the table among the other money. "I'll raise it a mite," he stated.

"You're licked right now, Redhead." Kelt Flecker grinned. It wasn't a nice grin and the rest of his features had nothing to do with it. But Knight wasn't finished yet. The play went around the table again. They waited for Knight to play.

Finally, Knight tossed his cards on the table. "That's all. There isn't any more."

Flecker asked, "You plumb cleaned?"

"I got one buck left to give my pony a decent feed."

"Put a price on him," Flecker said shortly.

Knight shook his head. "I won't let him go. You already gave me a price for my Winchester, so I could keep playing. Hell's-bells on a tomcat! You already won my rifle not to mention something close to two hundred bucks."

"You still got your six-gun," Flecker said slyly.

Knight considered; then, "What'll you give me for it?"

"Lemme see it."

Knight drew the well-worn six-shooter from holster and placed it on the table. Flecker examined it. "Good hawg-laig," he stated a bit reluctantly. "But it's a forty-four. We don't use them much around here. What you want to tote a forty-four for?"

"Same caliber as my rifle. This way I only have to carry one type cartridges."

Flecker nodded. "I'll allow you twenty bucks on this. Okay?"

"Okay," Knight sighed.

Flecker shoved two ten-dollar bills across the table.

The cards went around again. Needless to say,

Knight was cleaned out once more before the hand ended.

"Easy come, easy go," he smiled ruefully. "Now you can all go home. Maybe I could bed down in the livery stable loft, if the owner has a heart. Oh, well, I still got my bronc and rig." He added, forcing a grin, "Next thing, if I stick with you sharks, I'll be rolling home in a barrel. I arrived yesterday, a stranger in a strange land, and I been took in."

Beadle bridled. "You saying our game ain't run straight?"

Knight shook his head. "I wouldn't say that. Luck just didn't run my way. Usually an all-night game like this will bring a change of luck, two or three times, but it seems like I been on the skids for quite a spell."

"Sure, Tim, Knight didn't mean no harm," Flecker said. "He just proved to us he's a good loser. We ain't heard one yelp out of him." He considered a few moments. "After all, two hundred bucks and a shootin'-pole and hawg-laig is a lot to lose in one game. A saving of several months' wages, I'd guess."

He watched Knight narrowly while speaking, small shrewd eyes squinted narrowly.

Knight shrugged, meeting the look with a level glance that said nothing. He shrugged. "Could be," he confessed. "But then, wages come and go. I've got no kick coming. I wanted in on the game. It just wasn't my luck to win tonight. Maybe some other time I'll be able to pick up the cards I need."

Flecker sounded a bit over-eager: "You mean you can get hold of some cash, someplace?"

Jerry Knight laughed. "Well, I hope to—someday. Meantime, Flecker, you already guessed me as being a grub-line rider and saddle-tramp. So, what do you think? Maybe come beef-roundup I can tie on with some outfit. But don't mind me. You hombres go on with your game, unless you've had enough."

"Gawd! I had enough long ago." Tim Beadle yawned. "I want some breakfast and my bunk." His two companions echoed the words.

"Now, wait a minute," Flecker interposed quickly. "We'll play one more round. I'm still aiming to give Knight a chance to win back a few bucks. I don't want to see no waddie stoney-broke, and no job."

"Well, you'll just have to play without dealing me in—" Knight commenced.

"Wait a minute, I said," Flecker stated. "I'll stake you, Knight, for one hand."

"Hell, all I've got left is my togs and a part sack of Durham. You can't call that security for a loan. And I already told you I won't risk my pony and rig."

"You still got good security," Flecker pointed out.

Knight laughed scornfully. "What? My good rep? Another round with you hombres and you'd win that, too. Come to think of it, maybe that's not too good—anymore—either."

Herb Jacklin said, "Kelt, we're short a hand."

Flecker nodded thoughtfully. "Yeah, but I don't think Bristol Capron would stand for hiring one." Then to Knight, "What you figuring to do now?"

Knight said, "I've sort of been wondering about that myself. All's I seem to have left is my pony and my ambition. If anybody wants to hire an experienced cowhand for sale . . ." He paused without finishing the sentence.

"Look here"—Flecker seemed to have reached a sudden decision—"I'd really like to help you out, Knight, but the boss-man, Capron, has been after me to cut down expenses. We do need another man, but I can't find the wages to pay one. At the same time, I hate like hell to see the work get behind. Me, having the best interests of the Randall Land and Cattle Company at heart—which same hires both Capron and me—I'm aiming to try to stake 'em to the help needed."

"What you trying to say?" Knight asked curiously.

Flecker shoved four twenty-dollar bills across the table.

Knight eyed the money without picking it up. "Blast it," he stated a bit impatiently, "I already told you I haven't got any security to cover that."

"That's where you're wrong, waddie." Flecker laughed. "You got a carcass in good working order. I'm staking you to eighty bucks—the same being from your own roll, so you know they ain't counterfeit—"

"I'd sooner have my guns than that money—" Knight said.

"Forget the hardware." Flecker waved one careless hand. "Here's the proposition. You get eighty bucks. We'll deal one more hand. If you win, fine. You'll have a stake to go on. If you happen to lose, you sign a paper to me, agreein' to work for the Circle-F for a period of two months, without any pay, and I'll get a cowhand free gratis for nothing. You might even win the paper back too."

Knight grinned broadly. "Damn! You can't tie that for bigheartedness, Flecker."

"That's Kelt," Corwin put in. "Why, Knight, he'd give you the shirt off'n his back—"

"I already got a shirt," Knight commenced. "So—"

"—and he's a prime rod to ride for, too," Corwin finished.

"I reckon so," Knight said. He still appeared to hesitate before picking up the eighty dollars. "On the other hand, two months without any wages—"

"Cripes, man," Beadle said, "you get food and

bunk, anyway, for two months. By that time, beef-roundup should be due, and—"

"Jesus," Flecker stated impatiently. "I'll even give back your six-shooter and Winchester in the bargain." He placed the forty-four gun on the table. "Your rifle's standing against the wall behind you, when you want it. I don't aim to be greedy."

"That's more than decent." Knight appeared to weaken. "Hell!" he said abruptly. "Give me your paper. It's a deal."

Flecker smiled and drew from one pocket a small notebook in which he scribbled for a few minutes with a pencil stub. Tearing out the sheet, he pushed it across the table, with the pencil, to Knight. "Stick your moniker on that, waddie. Now, with a new start, we'll see if maybe your luck won't change."

Knight picked up the paper and scrutinized it. It was plainly worded, simply an agreement stating that one Jerry Knight gave his services to the Circle-F, for a period of two months, without pay, but including three meals a day and space in the bunkhouse, for the two months' period. Knight hadn't been able to find any catches, or double language, in the agreement, and with a flourish he signed the paper, pushed it back to Flecker.

"Let's go," he said.

Beadle was half asleep in his chair. Flecker shook him by the shoulder. "Come awake, Tim.

This is the last round." Beadle straightened in his chair. The cards were dealt around once more.

Play now seemed rather desultory. Bets at first were small. Beadle dropped out after the third round, Corwin was out after the fourth. Jacklin was good for only another round of betting. It now settled down to a battle between Flecker and Jerry Knight. They bet and raised, back and forth.

Twenty minutes later when the early rays of the sun sent a wide bank of yellow across the table, Flecker called, after Jerry Knight's last raise, which left him only a few dollars. He already knew he couldn't go on much longer.

"What have you got?" Knight asked.

Flecker showed his cards. Knight shrugged and tossed his hand on the table, face up.

"You win, Flecker," Knight stated calmly with a wry smile. "Three kings can top jacks and tens anytime."

"Tough luck, Knight." Flecker shook his head. "I reckon this just wasn't your night—and day." He smiled suddenly. "I'll be damned if this isn't the first time I ever won a man in a poker game."

"Anyway, Knight," Jacklin said, "you'll be workin' for one square foreman. That's something."

Corwin snickered. "Kelt's won just about everything except your good reputation, Knight."

"And I'd probably lost that if play had gone on." Knight smiled. "Anyway, could be he has to get one some place."

Flecker stiffened. "What you meaning by that, Knight?"

Jerry Knight stretched his arms and yawned. "We were talking about my rep as a poker player, weren't we? I reckon you got that."

"Oh, I see what you mean." Flecker relaxed again, though it wasn't quite clear in his mind what Knight had really meant. For a moment he considered the matter, then decided that Knight must have meant what he'd actually voiced. He twisted about in his chair and roused the napping Hippo.

"Hippo! Snap into it. A round of drinks all around on me. We're through playing."

Knight meanwhile had been gathering up the scattered cards and making them into a deck. Now he straightened in his chair, rose and started away with them toward the bar.

Flecker stiffened suddenly. "Where you going with them cards, Knight?"

Knight turned back, looking surprised. "Just returning them to Hippo. They're his cards, aren't they?"

Flecker's features cleared. "Oh, sure they're his. But we usually let him clear things up after we've left."

Hippodrome slid his comfortably upholstered

form from the stool and came around the bar, yawning, but coming awake.

He half stumbled against Knight on his way to the bar with the cards. "Hey," he mumbled sleepily, "you trying to run over me?"

"Running over you would be quicker than trying to go around." Knight chuckled, then added in a whisper, "Hang on to these cards, Hippo." And in a louder voice, "Make mine beer—colder the better."

Tossing the cards on the bar, Knight returned to the poker table.

"What a session you gents had," Hippodrome was saying when Knight again seated himself. "Criminey! A feller has to be a hound for draw to stick it that long. Who's the heavy winner?"

Knight nodded toward Flecker. "Kelt about cleaned up. These other boys aren't up to him when it comes to poker sharks. Me? I'm the loser, but it's a pleasure to lose to a real expert at the game. Damned if he didn't even win me."

"Won you?" Hippo looked blank.

Flecker explained, grinning broadly. Hippo sadly shook his head and took the orders. In a few minutes he was back with a tray. Knight scarcely tasted his beer. He was ready for breakfast, though not yet sure where it was to come from.

Corwin said, "If we can get ridin', maybe we can hit the Circle-F while there's still some warm fodder left."

Flecker shook his head. “I ain’t figuring to do no swift riding until I’ve et, not on no empty stomach. Anybody cravin’ to get his hoss at the livery stable is welcome to it if he wants to ride. I’m figurin’ we’ll eat at the Chinaman’s restaurant. And get this, I’m paying for the chow.”

“You must be feelin’ good this mornin’, Kelt,” Tim Beadle said.

“Well, I ain’t feeling mad at nobody, right now.” Flecker grinned. “C’mon, Knight, as a member of the crew you’re entitled to my free lunch too.”

Nodding good-byes to Hippodrome Casey, the five men sauntered to the door, unbolted it and stepped outside.

# III

Closing the door behind them, the men paused to glance along Topango Wells' main street. The sun was shining brightly now, and there was considerable warmth already in the air. Many citizens were abroad, taking down shutters and sweeping porches. At spots the sand was heaped seven or eight inches high against doors; windowsills and ledges everywhere were outlined with sand and dust. Waves of the gritty stuff lay in waves on roofs, such as could be seen.

The street was littered with rubbish and chunks of garbage, yellowed newspapers and tin cans, in those places where the street didn't resemble sand dunes on a seashore. Loose shingles lay here and there, and a couple of window shutters lay in the street. A good deal of profanity seemed to be issuing from the lips of those clearing up the mess. A few dogs were sniffing about and a half dozen chickens pecked futilely at the sandy wastes.

Glancing above, one would almost denied there'd been a Topango Howler last night and yesterday afternoon. The sky was a clear sapphire, except for a scattering of fleecy clouds chasing each other across the blue void.

“C’mon, let’s eat,” Flecker urged, impatiently. “I’m hungry.”

Jerry hesitated a moment as the men started again. “You hombres slope ahead down to the restaurant,” he suggested. “I’ll be with you in a minute.”

Flecker frowned suspiciously. “What you aimin’ to do, Knight?”

Knight explained: “I don’t want to tote this Winchester around. I’m going to stick it in my saddle-boot and see if my pony’s all right. Remember, I didn’t leave him in the livery stable like you hombres did. He’s around back of the saloon where I left him last night. I’ll be right along as soon as I see to him.”

Flecker hesitated. “But you don’t know where the restaurant is, Knight.”

Knight laughed. “In a town this size, I figure I can locate it. ’Sides, I ought to know. I was heading for there last evening when I rode in. But that time his sign blew off and nigh landed on me and the pony. Then his light blew out about the same time, so I continued on to Hippo’s place.”

Flecker nodded rather grumpily. “Oh, all right, but hurry up about it.”

He and his three hands continued off down the street, past the various buildings with high false-fronts, their booted feet clumping loudly along the plank sidewalks, the sounds being dulled where patches of drifted sand lay.

Jerry Knight rounded the corner of the saloon, passed between it and its neighboring building. At the rear of the Topango Saloon he found and filled a water bucket, then proceeded on to the horse shelter, where a wiry black gelding whinnied at his approach.

Watering the pony and filling a feed trough with food from a nearly empty sack that lay nearby required only a few moments more. His rifle had already been replaced in its boot. Leaving the horse, he entered through the now open rear door of the saloon.

Hippodrome Casey was yawning sleepily and polishing glasses when Knight stepped to the bar. A look of surprise crossed Hippo's rounded features.

"Cripes!" he said. "You back already? Thought you was eatin' breakfast."

Jerry Knight smiled, though an icy gleam had now entered his smoky gray eyes. "Figured you and I might as well get acquainted, Hippo. I won't keep you but a second."

Hippo looked uneasy. "What's on your mind, cowpoke? Let's get one thing straight: if you got cleaned out last night, I didn't have anything to do with it."

"I'm not saying you did. As to what's on my mind, right now I'm more interested in what's out of my pocket." Jerry smiled. "Hippo, Kelt Flecker's a right good poker player, isn't he?"

Hippodrome replied warily. "We-ell, I never did know him to lose with any regularity in the games he plays here. He's a hound for knowing the cards, rememberin' what cards has been dealt, and so on—"

"And how does he know so much?"

Hippodrome shrugged ponderous shoulders. "You got me."

"Yeah, I reckon, if I'm not wrong, he knows his cards in more ways than one. Hippo, let me see that deck of cards we were using."

"Thought you'd be coming up with somethin' like that," Hippo said caustically, "when you told me to save 'em. Cripes! They ain't nothin' wrong with them cards," he protested. "Knight, I myownself saw you break the seal on that pack, yourself, before you started play. Them's fairly expensive cards, too, made by a reliable company. Nothin' wrong with them cards."

"Just the same, I want to see 'em." Jerry's voice sounded rather peremptory.

Hippodrome hesitated, then reached below his bar and tossed the cards, in their cardboard case, onto the bar.

Jerry examined the broken seal, then gave a short laugh.

Hippo's bulky form stiffened a trifle. "That laugh sounded plumb nasty. What's up? Ain't them cards all right?"

"I haven't looked at the cards yet. Yeah, you're

right, Hippo, these cards were made by a reliable company. *But,* whoever steamed this seal off the cover, didn't replace it exactly as it was in the beginning. Take a look for yourself."

"B'God, you're right, Jerry," the fat barkeep conceded, after a minute inspection. "Now, what the devil—?"

"Devil's work, all right." Jerry could see the man's surprise was genuine, after gazing steadily at him a moment. "All right, Hippo, maybe you aren't in on this deal. We'll see what else we can learn."

Sliding the deck out of the case he scrutinized the backs of the pasteboards closely for several minutes.

Hippo asked, "What you lookin' for?"

"Marked cards. And I've found 'em. Nice examples of blockout work—"

"Block what?" Hippo looked puzzled. "What you talkin' 'bout?"

"Blockout work it's called."

Jerry Knight spread several of the cards face down on the bar.

"Look here. You'll see the pictures on the backs of these cards have a dog at either end. See? The dog's wearing a collar. These cards are printed in red on the backs. Now, take a close look at the dog collars on this Ace of Diamonds. Look close. See how someone has taken some red ink and filled in the white collars on the pups. It's right small—but it's there, when you know where to look. Study close. You won't have any trouble seeing it."

Hippo started to swear.

Jerry grinned. "Keep quiet, or your Sunday School teacher will spank you. Now, see this King of Clubs. Note how the dog's right forefoot has been blocked in with red. And here's a Queen of Spades, with the—"

Hippo exploded. "Why that goddamned, no-good, mangy son of a lousy rattler of a low-life!" He stared unbelievingly at the cards. "Any more blockouts?"

"Plenty." Jerry laughed. "Study 'em for yourself when you have time. Here and here"—swiftly pointing out cards—"and here's another. This deck is plenty sprinkled."

The fat man swore long and fervently. By now, Jerry was thoroughly convinced that the fat barkeep had had nothing to do with the swindle, or any hand at all in the deception.

Jerry asked, "Where'd these cards come from?"

"Kelt Flecker," Hippo exclaimed indignantly. "He's put one over on me."

"How come, Hippo?"

"Coupla years back," Hippo explained, "Kelt started kicking about the cards I kept here. They were cheap makes, I admit that, but good enough when fellers could use 'em for free. I fust kept 'em as a sort of 'commodation for fellers that wanted to play. Kelt's always goin' in for these all-night poker sessions, and he complained that my cards didn't stand up under long handlin'. Natural, I knew that, but I wasn't going to buy expensive brands."

"And so," Jerry put in shrewdly, "Kelt offered to furnish his own cards, for his own use, if you'd keep them here for him."

Hippo looked startled. "How in hell did you know that?"

"It's an old racket, my fat friend. It's been worked right frequent."

"I suppose so," Hippo said disgruntledly. "But wait—when would Kelt get a chance to mark them cards? Hell! He's even been cheatin' his own punchers. No wonder he always comes out winner."

"Kelt wouldn't have to mark the cards himself. There are several companies around that specialize in such work. Kelt just bought the cards from one of those outfits, then turned them over to you."

"God A'mighty, was anybody ever so dumb as me? Sa-a-ay, I'll bet I tell that bustard a thing or two. The crooked —"

"No, you won't. Listen, Hippo, you're not to say a thing about this. Keep quiet, and keep your eyes and ears open."

"Well, if I'm not to talk, and I don't know why, it's up to you, Jerry. Was I you I'd head right out and talk to Deputy-Sheriff Buck Drake. He's a square shooter—" He broke off. "How did you fall wise to this stuff?"

"I suspected it, after a few hands. Glanced at the backs of a couple of cards, then I was right sure, particularly in view of the fact the only time I could win was on small pots. When the kitty was plumb full, I was pretty sure to lose."

"Why in hell didn't you lodge a protest, 'stead of playing until Kelt cleaned you out. Looks like you're just a sucker."

"Could be." Jerry smiled. "But look, Hippo, what would have happened if I'd thrown the word 'cheating' during the game, and me playing against a foreman and three of his hands? They could have gunned me down in short order. I wouldn't have had a chance."

"You could have pulled out of the game."

"Maybe I didn't want to."

Hippo studied Jerry intently a few moments. "Look here, Jerry, what sort of game you playing?"

Jerry laughed shortly. "Look at it this way. If I lost, I figured I'd put Flecker under a certain obligation. I wanted a job on his spread. Now, I've got one."

Hippo looked somewhat disgusted. "Ask me, I've got an idea that your mind has completely lost its hobbles. You lost two hundred bucks for a chance to work two months for nothing. Hell!

I never heard nothing crazier. Well, you got a foot in the door anyway. Could be you'll be able to work yourself into a big job with the Randall Land and Cattle Company, some day."

"This Randall outfit swing much weight around here?"

Hippo nodded fatly. "They just about run things around Topango Wells—swallowing up everything in sight, land and cattle. Owned by some old crook back East. He never comes out here, but leaves things to his manager, Bristol Capron—got an office here. Flecker works for Capron, roddin' the Circle-F, which is one of the company's largest properties. Between Capron, resident manager, and Kelt Flecker, this range hereabouts is purty well made to toe the mark. No other outfit seems to have the guts to buck 'em."

"Sounds like a rough outfit to buck."

"You can bet your bottom dollar on that, Jerry. Me, I never say much myself, but I'm damned if I'm going to stand still for a crummy marked-card trick like Kelt is running. I always run a purty straight place. Live and let live is my motto, but if I don't spread the news about that slimy—"

"And catch yourself a lead slug in the brisket? Flecker would gun you down the minute you opened your trap. I've trusted you with what I've learned about those cards. Now, I'm asking, once more, please don't say anything about this."

Hippo said reluctantly, "We-ell, if you insist . . . but I don't like it. What are you aiming to do, Jerry?"

Jerry frowned. "I'm not sure yet what moves I'll make in the future. I've got a job with Flecker. That's a start. Maybe I'll just wait and see how he plays his cards. Actually, I think he was really anxious to take me on. His bighearted palaver didn't fool me one minute—"

The words were interrupted by a hail from the street. It was Tim Beadle's voice. Before the man had a chance to open the saloon door, Jerry pushed marked cards and case to the floor behind the bar.

# IV

As the cards landed at Hippodrome's feet, he looked puzzled for a moment, then realized that Knight hadn't wanted Beadle to learn they had been discussing the pasteboards. He gave a short approving nod, as Beadle pushed open the door.

"Hey, Knight, what you think you're doin'?" he demanded in surly tones.

Knight glanced around. "Oh, hello, Beadle. Through breakfast, already—?"

"What in hell you waitin' around here for?" Beadle snapped. "You said you'd show up right away."

"I know, I know," Jerry said placatingly, "but I was detained longer than I expected—"

"Maybe that won't go down with Kelt. He don't like to be crossed. He got an idea you might of run out on your agreement with him, and—"

Jerry gave a soft laugh. "No need for Flecker to get his sit-spot in a tizzy. I had no intention of running for it."

"Well, what held you up? What you doin' in here?"

"No particular reason you shouldn't know—nor Flecker either. I just stopped a minute to see if Hippo would have any balsam of fir, or turpentine, or maybe some powdered ginger or sulphur. 'Course, he didn't, but there was a chance—"

Tim Beadle's jaw dropped. He commenced to look bewildered. "Balsam of fir? Turpentine? Ginger? Sulphur? What in hell you talkin' about?"

"Good for the heaves," Jerry explained.

"Heaves?" Beadle appeared flabbergasted. "Who's got the heaves?"

Jerry grinned. "For a minute I thought maybe you had, when you come bellerin' in here." He explained: "Sorry I kept you waiting, but my pony was acting like he had the heaves when I went back to look after him. I fooled around with him a mite. After I wet down his fodder some, he quit that sort of coughing he got, every time he breathed. I reckon he'll come along all right. Might be the livery or general store can supply those remedies I mentioned, if he don't."

"So what if he doesn't?" Beadle growled. "You can always get another bronc. Hell, I've seen hosses act like that before, after a Topango Howler hits town—all that grit and sand in the air. Or maybe there was some chaff or dust in his feed."

"Could be," Jerry conceded.

Beadle swung testily on Hippo. "You, Hippo, you should have told Knight that Kelt doesn't like to be kept waitin'."

Hippo bridled, face growing red. "T'hell you

say, Tim. If you figure I'm going to ride herd on every stranger that hits this town, you got another bit of figurin' to do. If you don't like the way I run things here, you can—"

"Take it easy, Hippo." Jerry laughed, though the tones earned a certain warning. "Tim doesn't mean anything. Flecker, like's not, has been taking out his mad at me on Tim, and he's still fretted at something that was all my fault. C'mon, Tim, we'll get along to the restaurant."

He nodded good-bye to Hippo and passed out to the street with Beadle.

On the way, Jerry said, "You hombres finished eating sooner than I expected."

"I don't know what you expected, but we did," Beadle said sourly. "Except for Kelt. He's still eatin'. Never knew a man who could stow away so much grub as him. He was on his third order of steak and eggs, when he sent me to find you."

"Cripes! I didn't know I was under orders."

"Well, you'd best learn it right now, then," Beadle snapped. "You work for Kelt and you're under orders all the time—night and day. And he don't like to be crossed. He's good-natured up to a certain point. After that, he'd just as soon lift your scalp as look at you. He can be goddamn mean at times."

"That so?" Jerry laughed shortly. "He won't be lifting no scalp of mine."

"Now don't you get proddy, Knight. He'll lift it

and make you like it, any time the idea hits him. He's plumb bad medicine to buck, and in your position, you'd best build your loops just as he tells you to."

"What do you mean—in my position?"

Beadle gave a short sarcastic laugh. "All right, Knight, don't admit to nothing you don't have to—but there's some things you don't have to admit to Kelt—things he already knows. But if you don't play the game to Kelt's liking, you ain't going to relish what'll happen, *sabe*?"

"I'm damned if I do."

Beadle shrugged and rubbed his lantern-jaw. "Have it your way, cowpoke. I won't say no more, but I'm just warnin' you, you won't be able to run no bluff on Kelt Flecker."

The men strode on, passing on the way a two-story building with the front painted in sun-faded and peeling lettering, RANDALL LAND & CATTLE COMPANY. Jerry noted that the shutters hadn't yet been taken down, and a heap of sand was piled against the front door, which was closed tightly.

"That the place that runs things around here?" Jerry asked.

Beadle glanced toward the building. "Yeah," he answered. "Bristol Capron, the manager, lives upstairs. Office downstairs. He's the only hombre Kelt takes orders from, and sometimes I've wondered if it wasn't the other way around.

Kelt, mostly, seems to do as he likes." As if he'd said too much Beadle clamped shut his lips once more and just shrugged when Jerry asked further questions.

The two men crossed diagonally to the restaurant across the street. The sign that had blown down the previous night was now standing against the front wall of the low building. The Chinaman had swept the porch, which was raised two steps above ground level. Within the restaurant was a long counter, fronted by stools. Four unoccupied tables stood across the room.

Kelt Flecker was occupied with a huge chunk of pie and a cup of coffee when Beadle and Knight entered. Seated on stools at the counter with him, were Corwin and Jacklin, smoking brown paper cigarettes. Behind the counter stood a neat, smiling-faced Oriental.

"Here he is, Kelt," Beadle announced.

Flecker twisted on his stool, a dribble of food falling from one corner of his mouth. There was a splash of egg-yellow on his shirt and empty dishes were ranged before him.

"Where in hell you been, Knight?" he roared through a mouthful of food. "Thought you'd run out on me."

Jerry explained, telling the story he'd related to Beadle.

Flecker nodded when he had concluded. He appeared placated. "Aw, your bronc'll be all right. If he ain't, we got plenty mounts out at the Circle-F. Ain't much difference in hosses. Beat 'em over the head with the end of a loaded quirt, and they'll learn to behave. Jest like a woman in that respect." He guffawed and swung back to his pie and coffee. "Sit down and eat hearty. Better fodder here than you'll get at the Circle-F."

Jerry settled himself on a stool and ordered ham, fried eggs, fried *frijoles*, biscuits, pie and coffee. The smiling Chinese took his order and vanished in the direction of the kitchen. The food arrived in short order, hot and tasty, and Jerry fell to, while Flecker was ordering more pie and coffee.

George Corwin observed, "Kelt, you eat like a hoss."

"Why shouldn't he?" Jerry paused eating to inquire. "This is good stable food."

The three punchers looked blank but a sudden guffaw from Flecker sent bits of pie across the counter. "What a joke!" Flecker exploded. "See—hoss, stable?" explaining to his three punchers, who smiled slightly. "Knight, I'll bet you didn't realize you was makin' a joke."

"Hey, that is sort of funny, isn't it?" Jerry said and returned to his platter.

The door opened and a tall, thin man in citizen's clothing entered. His head was almost devoid of hair and his eyebrows were sparse. He had a long beaked nose and a tight mouth. In short, his was the face of a predatory vulture. He frowned on seeing Flecker and the other punchers.

"Mornin', Mr. Capron," Flecker said. "You look like you just got out of your bed."

"True enough," the man said, in thin nasal tones. "Couldn't sleep with the wind howling like it was. Didn't shut my eyes until near daylight. What you doing in town so early?"

"Ain't left since yesterday," Flecker replied through a mouthful of pie. "Think we'd be fools enough to ride back in that gale?" Then to Jacklin, "Herb, find another stool. I want Mr. Capron to sit next to me."

Jacklin found another seat. Capron seated himself and gave the Chinese his order. A half dozen other customers drifted in from the street. Jerry continued eating; he was nearly finished now.

Jerry heard Flecker say, "Mr. Capron, I signed on a new hand last night—Knight, by name. That redheaded galoot a few stools down."

Capron gave Jerry a sharp glance, nodded shortly, and turned a trifle testily on Flecker. "Flecker," he snapped, "I thought I gave you orders to do no more hiring—"

"I know, I know," Flecker said. "But we need another man. Knight's a good cowpoke, knows his business. Might even be prime for doctorin' stock too. Why, just this mornin' he was trying to get some sulphur to cure his hoss of the heaves—

sulphur and turpentine and God knows what else—"

"Regardless," Capron interrupted harshly, "I told you—"

"Let be a minute, Mr. Capron." Flecker spoke to his crew. "You boys hike out to the porch and enjoy the sunshine. Knight, you look like you was finished. Go ahead with 'em and roll yourself a smoke. I want to talk private to Mr. Capron a few minutes."

Obediently the men arose. Jerry drained his coffee cup and followed the others to the porch outside the restaurant. They waited there, rolling and lighting Bull Durham cigarettes.

In the restaurant, Flecker and Bristol were talking in low tones. Capron was shaking his head. "I don't like it, Flecker. We can't push our luck too far. Should the company ever decide to send an auditor out here, now that—"

"Take it easy—"

"Maybe I've been taking it easy too long. Sometimes it worries me. We should be more careful than ever, now that—"

"Will you just leave things to me?" Flecker said.

"But face the truth, Flecker. Another man just means we're padding the payroll more. You've already got three hands out at the ranch that don't begin to earn their pay, and—"

"I haven't forgotten it." Flecker's face darkened. "I've been studyin' those hombres a mite. They don't look to me like they'd play the game with us. Once beef-roundup is over, I'm figurin' to give 'em the sack—"

"Even so, this Knight fellow—"

"Isn't going to cost the company a cent, Capron. I got a paper signed by him that says, clear, he'll work for us two months without pay."

"Without pay?" Capron looked astounded. "I can't believe it."

"I'm tellin' you. He wanted a job bad. I busted him in a poker game last night—plumb cleaned him out. Then I staked him to another hand on condition he donate two months' work if he lost the pot. He lost. This way he gets a bunk and chow." Flecker concluded, giving details.

Capron looked dubious. "Something fishy there, I'm afraid."

"Hell, he's like all cowpokes—strong back and weak mind. He's just plain dumb, I tell you. No man, less'n he's plain stupid, would stay in a game until he's entirely cleaned out, and then agree to work two months without wages."

"But do you think he can be trusted?" Capron sipped from his cup.

Flecker laughed. "He better damned well be trusted. Look, Capron, I know enough about Knight to put him in a jail cell right now."

Capron's brow cleared a trifle. "Oh, you knew him before?"

"I knew of him. The law wants him. 'Sides that, I figure he'll make a right nice picture."

"Picture?" Capron frowned, and took another drink of coffee, then ordered a cigar from the Chinese. When it was placed before him, he nodded suddenly. "Oh, you mean he's a good object for framing."

"Exactly. We've got to do something. That damned Deputy-Sheriff Buck Drake keeps snooping around, still trying to locate the third man in—"

"Shh!" Capron said quickly. "No need putting it into words. I know what you mean. So you figure Knight will make a good suspect."

"Why not? Any man who thinks more of his hoss than he does his own skin, just don't know which end of a throw-rope is the *hondo* end. The hombre's brain, if it was dynamite, there ain't enough of it to blow off his Stet hat. Believe me, I know what I'm talkin' about."

"All right, Flecker. I'll just have to leave it to you." He lighted his cigar, exhaled a cloud of gray smoke. "But speaking of dynamite, I've had a feeling we're sitting on a keg of the stuff with the fuse lighted, for some time now, ever since Deputy Buck Drake showed he hasn't given up trying to find the man—"

"And now it's your turn not to be putting anything in words. Just remember, I can handle anything that comes up, just like I always have."

He beckoned to the Chinese and paid him for the breakfasts.

The two men conversed in low tones a few minutes more, then Kelt Flecker said good-bye and rose to join his men on the porch, a chunk of steak falling from his lap as he rose from the stool.

On the restaurant porch he said to Jerry and the others, “Reckon we’d best be gettin’ started for home. There’s a long day ahead of us yet.”

Jerry started down off the porch and headed toward the Topango Saloon.

Flecker called after him. “Knight, where in hell you headed now?”

“Aiming to get my pony. You hombres have to get your broncs at the livery, don’t you? I’ll be waiting for you when you come past.”

“See that you’re there, that’s all,” Flecker said grumpily.

# V

Horses were mounted and the five riders swept west out of Topango Wells, taking the most central of several trails, rutted and wheel-chopped, that fanned out beyond the town. Off to the southwest, the grass was sparse, the terrain largely sandy-waste.

Jacklin, Corwin and Beadle had spurred somewhat ahead, leaving Flecker and Jerry Knight riding fairly close together. Flecker jerked one thumb toward the southwest. "Yonderly," he commented, "is where them fool hoe-men are figurin' to make crops. Now any fool can see you don't grow nothing there 'less'n you aim to raise cactus and salt-bush. But them idiots don't know no better, I reckon. Now if they had reg'lar supplies of water . . ." He spat a long brown stream of tobacco juice disgustedly and let the words remain unfinished.

"What do you cowmen do for water?" Knight asked.

"That's no problem." Flecker and Knight were moving at an easy lope now; the others still farther ahead. "There's a right smart little stream cuts down from the hills between Circle-F holdin's and the Two-M spread, owned by old man Mart Monroe. And there's waterholes spotted here and there. Fine grazin' too. The few other spreads to the northwest have plenty of water too, though they're just small outfits."

"I take it, then, that the Circle-F and Two-M are the biggest outfits hereabouts," Knight commented.

"Correct—only we're the biggest," Flecker replied pridefully. "Time ain't far off when the Circle-F will swallow up the Two-M too—"

"And then the small outfits?" Knight asked curiously.

"Right. Don't get me wrong. We'll do it all hunky-dory—buy 'em out in legal shape."

Knight nodded, but he was beginning to wonder exactly how legal such deals would be.

Ahead of him now he could see, more sharply etched against the blue sky, rolling grazing lands, rising to low hills. The way became less arid and grasslands began to appear—lush grama grass—with here and there mesquite trees or an occasional prickly pear cactus. Now and then a sage hen, or chaparral cock, darted out of growth to flash across the path of the riders. They began to see white-faced Hereford cows, branded on the left flank with the Circle-F brand and swallow-fork earmarks. Many of them were standing in the shade of huge outcroppings of gray granite, rising above their heads.

"Prime looking critters," Knight observed, when they'd passed one bunch.

Flecker agreed. "Nobody raises 'em better'n the Randall outfit. Ain't much about fattenin' cows I don't know"—adding modestly—" 'course I got to give some credit to the good grazin' 'round here. Ain't no better spot in the whole cow-country for raisin' fine beef."

"I'm surprised," Jerry Knight said, "that the outfit's not called the Circle-R—for Randall—rather than Circle-F. What's the F stand for?"

"Man named Fremont once owned the outfit. His beef had a good rep back East, clear to Kansas City, so when old man Randall bought him out, he decided to keep the same brand. Not a bad idea, neither."

"I was thinking that," Knight observed shrewdly.

The words were casually spoken, but something in Jerry's tone brought a sharp look from Kelt Flecker. He thought it over a few moments, then asked rather sharply, "Exactly what you meanin', Knight?"

"Just what you said," Jerry evaded.

"You had something else in mind," Flecker accused.

"Did I?" Knight asked innocently.

"Well, it sounded like it to me." Flecker scowled. "Exactly, what were you hintin' at?"

"Just an idea," Jerry confessed. "I was thinking, say, if you weren't an honest foreman, how easy it would be to round up a few Randall cows and change brands—say, make the F into an E, or maybe an 8—"

"What do you know about blottin' brands?" Flecker glowered.

"Damn little. Just what I've heard tell from fellers."

"All right," Flecker said tartly, "for the sake of argument, let's say I'm not honest—which same I am, of course—"

"Of course."

"—and I did change the brands from an F to an E or 8," Flecker continued. "What then? What could I do with 'em?"

"Herd 'em over the county line to some strange territory—or even into Mexico, which can't be too far from here. Then furnish phony bills of sale for the changed brands to some cowman who didn't care where his stock come from, and put the money in your own pocket."

"Huh," Flecker grunted. He didn't speak again for a few minutes while the horses loped slowly on. His brow was gathered in a frown. "Y'know"—he spoke finally, bluntly—"maybe you ain't as big a fool as I figured you was."

Jerry laughed. "Maybe I couldn't be, Kelt. Oh, don't give me credit for smart thinking. I heard one time of a stunt like that being pulled up in Oklahoma."

Flecker looked somewhat relieved. "Well, anyway, I could never get away with a dirty trick like that on my boss. That Bristol Capron is sharp. He keeps books. Knows right to the last count how many cows we should have. He's right strict 'bout things like that."

"The owner ever come out here?" Jerry asked.

"Who, old man Randall? I've never seen him. He leaves everything to Bristol Capron. It was Capron that hired me, some years back. Good man to work for, but inclined to be a mite sour at times, if he gets crossed. . . . Knight, where did you say you'd worked before?"

Jerry told him.

"Yeah, you told me those brands before. Like I said I never heard of 'em. You ever been in any trouble—rustlin' and such like, Knight?"

"Never rustled a cow in my life—"

"What other trouble then?"

"I didn't say I'd ever been in any ruckus. Me, I'm peaceful, I am. I don't like trouble. Y'know, a feller can get arrested if he makes trouble for folks. I've always aimed to steer shy of the law."

"A lot of stick-up men stay clear of the law, too, as long as they can," Flecker said slyly.

"I reckon. Never gave that end of it much thought. I saw a feller hung once, and for nothin' more than killin' another hombre in a card game. Can you imagine that?"

Again, Flecker didn't reply at once, but Jerry thought he heard him mutter under his breath: "Yep, dumb as dishwater."

They rode on, mile after mile slipping easily beneath the horses' hooves. They'd picked up a bit more speed by this time. Already, riding fast, the other three were far ahead. Now they were ascending slightly rising terrain. And then, Jerry suddenly caught sight of the ranch buildings, nestled between two low hills, with cottonwood trees and brush scattered about the outskirts. Before long he could hear the clanking of a windmill as it moved slightly in the light breeze. Gradually they closed in and swept into the ranch-yard.

The buildings were large and in good condition, built partly of frame and partly of adobe. There was a low ranch house fronted by a long gallery, at present not in use, with doors and windows boarded up. There was a blacksmith shop, corrals, a big barn, and a cook shanty, adjacent to a long bunkhouse of frame and adobe construction. Flecker bunked with his men, and had a sort of office installed at one end. Knight noticed, as he rode past, three cowhands seated on a top rail of one of the corrals, containing a number of saddle ponies.

Flecker and Jerry slowed near the corral. Flecker yelled at the three seated on the corral rail: "One of you cow-nurses, strip off our rigs, and take care of the hosses."

A cowhand climbed down from the corral rail. Flecker and Jerry stepped to the ground.

Jerry said, "I can take care of my own pony—"

Flecker cut him short: "Let them do it. They're just deadwood round here anyway—lazy as hell." He made no effort to keep his tones down. "Come on, Knight."

Jerry seized his slim bed-roll from behind his saddle and the rifle from its boot and followed Flecker into the bunkhouse, after dropping reins over his pony's head.

Within the bunkhouse, a series of double-tiered bunks ran along one wall. There were windows in front and back walls. A long board table, at present littered with old magazines and newspapers, a broken spur, two pieces of broken harness and other odds and ends, at either side of which was a long bench, stood in the center of the room. At the far end was a rough board desk and chair with arms, which Flecker was pleased to term his "office," at present holding a few pencil stubs and a ranch tally book. A few old calendars from packing companies decorated the walls.

Flecker indicated several vacant bunks, holding only straw-filled mattresses. "Take your pick," he told Jerry, "and call it home."

Jerry said, "Well, you sound right hospitable, anyway, Kelt."

"Anybody signs up with me gets prime treatment, Knight. Once your two-months without pay is ended, I aim to start payin' you regular wages. I figure you're goin to want to stay here.

It'll make a good hideout for you." He laughed craftily.

"Hideout?" Jerry asked.

"I reckon you know what I mean." Flecker leered. "If not, you'd best think it over a mite."

To Jerry there seemed to be a certain threat in the words. He didn't pursue the subject, deciding to wait for further developments. He glanced about the bunkhouse, noting that Corwin, Jacklin and Beadle were already in their bunks, snoring lustily. They'd not even bothered to remove their boots, but slept with their sombreros covering their faces.

Flecker crossed the floor and sat down on his own bunk and started tugging off his boots and shirt. "I'm aimin' to join that snorin' concert right pronto," he announced. "You'd best do the same, Knight. We all missed a lot of shut-eye last night."

"But when do I start work?" Jerry protested.

"Tomorrow mornin'," Flecker replied promptly, stretching out in his bunk and arranging a blanket. "I'm takin' it easy today, and you'd best do likewise. I ain't hard on my hands, Knight—providin' they always follow orders I give 'em. Understand?"

There was something ominous in the words, but Jerry appeared to ignore Flecker's attitude. He nodded shortly. "I've always been able to take orders any place else I've worked, Kelt."

"That's hunky-dory. Keep on doin' that way, and you and me won't never have no trouble. Oh, yeah, before you turn in, you'd best drift down to the cook shanty and tell cookie he'll have an extra gut to feed tonight—and I don't want to be waked up for no dinner. I'll make up for that when we have supper."

# VI

Jerry crossed to the open doorway of the bunk-house and for several minutes stood gazing thoughtfully across the range, gray eyes narrowed in cogitation. His lips tightened as certain possibilities coursed his mind. He turned back to his bunk, delved into his bed-roll, then returned to resume his stance at the doorway, taking the opportunity to replenish the empty loops in his cartridge belt with fresh loads. He glanced once at Flecker's prone form in the bunk, but by this time the man was puffing and snorting as loudly as the other three sleepers.

"Flecker," Jerry told himself, "seems damned confident. To me it looks as though I might run into trouble before long, if things break the wrong way—and at present it doesn't look as though they're headed in any other direction."

Thus the thoughts swirled through his mind as he remained in the doorway a few minutes longer, then he stepped out and made his way to the cookhouse. The kitchen proved typical of many such places: pots, pans and kettles were suspended on hooks in one wall, near a big cast-iron stove with oven. Stacked firewood was piled nearby. Dishes and cups, mostly of tin, were ranged on shelves. Open cupboards disclosed sacks of potatoes, beans, flour and canned goods. A slab of bacon and another of "sow-belly" hung from ceiling hooks. There was a wooden table and a straight-back chair.

Both chair and table were occupied at the moment: the table by several flour sacks, employed as dishtowels, and a partly filled bottle of whisky and tumbler; the chair, by a wizened individual with a bald head, long red nose and a sweeping dirty-gray moustache. The cook wore faded jeans, a woolen shirt and ordinary scuffed leather boots.

This individual cocked a somewhat bleary blue eye as Jerry's footstep sounded at the door. "Who in tarnation hell," he demanded sourly, "invited you into my kitchen? And get it into your head, right now, I ain't got no handouts for saddle-tramps."

"Now don't get proddy, grandpaw," Jerry advised, chuckling.

"And I ain't nobuddy's grandpaw, I'll have you know," the old cook stated wrathfully. "My names Jones—Cornpone Jones—Mister Jones, to you. And what did—?"

"Don't tell me!" Jerry beamed. "Why, say, Mister Jones, I've heard of you. This must be my lucky day—"

"What you mean, your lucky day? An' what did you ever hear 'bout me?—and mind you—I ain't goin' to make up no sourdough and beef sandwich at this hour—what was it, you heared 'bout me?"

"Your biscuits! You're the cook that makes such light biscuits, you just have to open the oven door and they float out of their own accord. Isn't that right?"

Cornpone Jones appeared somewhat mollified. He almost smiled. "If I do say it myself, I do turn out a right tasty biscuit, when I set my mind to it," he said in his squeaky tones. "Sorry I ain't got none to hand, right this minute. But what did you want to see me 'bout, waddie?"

"My name's Knight—Jerry Knight. Kelt told me to come and tell you he took me on—"

"T'hell he did! Another hungry mouth to feed, I suppose." The sour manner was returning. "What Kelt took you on for, is more'n I can say. He needs 'nother hand 'bout as much as a cow needs extra horns. I suppose you been ridin' grub-line—"

"Something like that." Jerry smiled. "Well, I'll see you come chow time, *Mister* Jones."

Without giving the ancient cook time to say anything more, he backed out of the doorway.

Outside once more, he stood wondering what to do next. He glanced down toward the saddlers' corral and saw the three punchers were still there, though now they'd left the top rail and were standing on the ground. He realized they'd been surreptitiously sizing him up and trying to figure who he was and what he was doing at the Circle-F.

He approached easily and spoke to them. They nodded genially enough. Jerry said, “My name’s Knight—Jerry Knight.”

One of them thrust out his hand. “My moniker’s Steve Hackett. These other hombres are Shorty Wing and Frank Reed. Glad to make your acquaintance, Knight.” Jerry shook hands with the other two men.

All three were young, good-featured, bronzed sons of the cattle country. Hackett had good eyes and a firm jaw. Reed was a rather quiet type, with wide shoulders and blond hair. Shorty Wing, as to be suspected, was short but with a barrel-like chest and a penetrating glance.

“You ropin’ for the Circle-F, now—or just a friend of Kelt’s?” Hackett asked quietly.

“We-ell,” Jerry replied, “I can’t say I’m any particular friend of Flecker’s. On the other hand, he hired me for the Circle-F crew.”

Shorty Wing swore, said to his companions, “Can you top that, hombres? One more hand for this outfit?”

The other two looked rather skeptical. Jerry asked, “What’s wrong with hiring another hand, here?” He’d already noted that these three cowhands, men about his own age, lacked the hard-bitten look of Flecker and his three cronies. He felt, if necessary, these three could be trusted.

Reed said warily, "Actually, Knight, things are a mite dull right now. The herds don't need too much attention—Kelt and the other three do much of the work in that line. What Kelt keeps us for is a mystery to me. Mostly we just work around here, whitewashin' buildin's, diggin' water tanks out on the range, taking care of the broncs when it's necessary. There ain't even none left to be topped off—"

"Easiest job I ever had," Shorty Wing told Jerry. "I ain't been in a saddle for nigh two weeks now. Kelt keeps us three at tinkerin' jobs—mendin' harness and settin' corral posts and the like. For all we do, we might just as well join them hoe-men off to the south. Them poor bustards work hard enough."

"What hoe-men?" Jerry asked innocently.

"Some dry-farmers south of Aliso Creek," Wing explained.

"I'm strange to this range," Jerry hinted.

"Sure enough you are." Wing had freckles and they showed up more when he smiled. "I'd forgot that. Well, you see, the Randall Land and Cattle Company have a lot of farms staked out to sell to suckers over that way. Them poor benighted hoe-men come out from the Midwest and aim to become dirt farmers. Cripes! They can't hardly raise enough to keep from starvin'. When Aliso Creek's up they get fair irrigation, but come hot weather the creek peters out and crops is ruined."

Jerry's gray eyes narrowed. "I should think it would pay to dam up the creek and save water for when it gets hot."

"And who's to pay for that?" Frank Reed asked.

"The Randall Company, of course," Jerry replied promptly. "If they sell the land, they're obligated, as I see it—"

A chorus of derisive laughs greeted the statement. "That's a joke too," Hackett said scornfully. "Hell, Knight, that's part of the Randall Company's game. Sell the land to suckers, then when they can't keep up payments, foreclose and sell to more suckers—"

Frank Reed said cautiously, "Better put a button on that lip, Steve. Flecker might not like things of that sort bandied about."

"That ain't no skin off'n my teeth," Hackett said scornfully. "If Flecker don't like what I say, I'll tell him to go bark at himself—"

"Could be," Hackett replied, "he's the type that might do his barking with a six-shooter. You ain't no match with him, Steve."

"Regardless," Hackett said doggedly. "Shucks, just as soon as I collect me a couple more months' wages, I'm aimin' to pull out."

"Me, too," from Shorty Wing. "I just don't like the way things is shapin' up, around here."

Hackett drew a long sigh, then said, "Well, if you hombres insist on talkin' out loud, I'll say no more. To tell the truth, I don't like it either."

The men fell silent and rolled brown paper cigarettes with sacks of Bull Durham. Jerry tried to reopen the subject. "If that's the way the Randall Company treats the dirt farmers, it looks like a dirty deal to me."

"You think so, too?" Shorty Wing looked pleased.

"I sure do. I think it's something that ought to be taken up with Bristol Capron—I understand he's the resident manager."

"Jest try it, Knight," Reed said quietly, "if you're aimin' to face a chunk of Flecker's lead. Capron don't do nothing without Flecker agreein'. I mentioned the business of the hoe-men to Flecker once, and he nigh bit my head off. So I've learned to keep my trap shut, after he told me to keep out of things that wasn't none of my business. He claims that he has to take his orders from Capron, and he don't ask Capron no questions. I figure him as a liar."

"There's somethin' funny goin' on," Hackett put in. "Knight, I can't see why he hired you—" He stopped abruptly, then said, "Maybe I do, though—" and again stopped. "Just forget I said anything," he added apologetically. "Sure, Knight, we like our jobs fine. What say we drop the subject?"

Jerry smiled. "I don't talk much and I never did make a habit of repeating what I hear."

"Kind of sized you up that way, at first." Wing

smiled sheepishly. “Could be that’s why we all blurted out a lot of talk.”

“As I said, I don’t talk much,” Jerry said. “I’m just interested to see what I’ve got into. You boys seemed agreed that something queer is going around. My curiosity is aroused. Exactly what do you think is off-color?”

Shorty Wing frowned. “You tell me and I’ll tell you. You see, this Randall that owns practically everything hereabouts, lives in the East—Kansas City, I think. He leaves everything to Capron. I get to wonderin’ sometimes if Capron wouldn’t like to run the company in a hole of some sort—”

“And then, what?”

Wing shrugged broad shoulders. “I ain’t thought that out, ’sides the possibility of Capron runnin’ some crooked records in his accounts. On the other hand, it looks like the Randall Company is out to hog the whole country hereabouts. It holds notes on some of the ranches, way north of here, and nearer, and I’ve heard that said ranches is losin’ cows—more’n they can afford to lose. Now, mind, I ain’t got no proof of this—”

“Where’d you get your information?” Jerry wanted to know.

“Just rumors I picked up when I was in Topango Wells, from time to time. All hearsay, you might figure.”

“How about outfits nearer the Circle-F—who are they?”

“The Rafter-K is about fifteen miles due north from Topango Wells. The Coffee-Pot about the same distance to the northeast. I understand both owe money to the Randall outfit. Then southwest of here, beyond the foothills, lies the Two-M, owned by old Mart Monroe. Their holdin’s sort of form a boundary line next to the Circle-F, in a due west direction. They got quite a spread, nigh as large as the Circle-F.”

“Randall Company holding some of their notes, too, I expect,” Jerry commented.

“Nope. I don’t figure so,” Wing replied. “Old Monroe is a right sharp customer, got a dang pretty daughter, too, and a good crew of hands. I’ve a hunch that Randall would like to have a finger in that pie, but Monroe is mighty independent. Him and his men don’t seem to want to have anything to do with the Circle-F. They ain’t uppity—them I’ve seen in Topango Wells—but on the other hand, they sorta mind their own business and make it plain they won’t take no pushin’ around.”

“If ever a range war should erupt,” Frank Reed put in, “I’d figure it would be between the Circle-F and the Two-M.”

Jerry asked, “Does the Circle-F make money on its beef?”

“It should,” Steve Hackett answered promptly, “though I don’t know what price it gets. There was a mighty big shipment went east last fall.”

"Just one trainload?" Jerry wanted to know.

"There was several," from Shorty Wing. "Hell! The Circle-F has herds scattered all over—even to the extent of mixin' with other brands sometimes. Flecker has had complaints about that, but it don't appear to fret him none."

"Anyway," Jerry said shrewdly, "it doesn't look like the Circle-F suffers any shortages."

"Never heard tell of any"—Hackett shrugged—"though I can't speak for certain. I don't get into a saddle to know much what is going on. You'll have to ask Flecker or one of them hands that are close to him. And that goes for Shorty and Frank, too. Why you askin'?"

"Put it down to being curious." Jerry smiled. "But if some ranches complain of losing stock, it's a wonder some owner hasn't called on the Cattlemen's Association to send an investigator out here to look around a mite and do some snooping."

"Could be somebody did." Wing frowned and then continued, "There was a hombre named Wolcott come here about three months back—"

"Range detective?" Jerry asked.

"I don't know for sure. Wolcott never talked much to anybody. Just did a heap of ridin', roamin' around the range. And then it ended sudden—"

Jerry asked quickly, "What happened?"

Wing drew a deep breath. "Nobody rightly

knows. Wolcott was found dead—shot to death in the back—some miles to the west of here. A cowhand that had worked for the Circle-F—Ridge Conway—was found dead, too, a few yards away from him. Conway was a mean cuss. But it was figured that the two shot it out for some reason—"

"With Wolcott shot in the back?' Jerry asked skeptically.

"Fishy explanation, eh?" Frank Reed put in, nodding. "But Flecker says he thinks that Conway had enough strength to fire one more shot before he died, at a moment when Wolcott's back was turned. No, he claimed he didn't know what they scrapped about, but a lot of folks accept Flecker's explanation."

"Don't they all?" Jerry asked.

"Not Deputy-Sheriff Buck Drake," Steve Hackett said. "He's still going around, asking questions."

"Well, does that pin anything on the Circle-F?" Jerry asked.

"It ain't for me to say." Frank Reed spoke, scowling. "Like Steve said, the deputy-sheriff is still investigating—mostly because it was known that Flecker and Conway was right close. Though later, Flecker claimed him and Conway had had a falling-out over a hoss trade, two days before the bodies were found. Flecker also stated, at an inquest, that Conway had quit his job directly after the falling-out. Here's something else: Wolcott had been winged in the shoulder—from the front—by a forty-five slug—maybe Conway's. But it was the slug between the shoulder blades that killed him."

Jerry nodded slowly. "To me that proves that Conway had a pal with him—maybe hidden out behind some rocks or brush, and between them they got Wolcott—even if Wolcott got Conway first."

"Something like that." Shorty Wing nodded. "Deputy-Sheriff Drake is still trying to uncover that third man, but I reckon he's not having much success."

Jerry gave a short laugh, but there was small amusement in it. "Sure looks like a fine outfit I've signed on with."

"Well, you can always quit," Shorty pointed out.

"Not this time, I can't. I signed up for two months' work with no wages."

The other three stared unbelievingly at him. Reed said, "Well, you must have been awful hard up for a job."

"Maybe I was." He considered the matter of confiding a minute, then said, "It was this way. I'm sort of dumb at times—understand?" From that point on he related what had happened, the all-night poker game and so on, supplying various details as he went along. When he had concluded, the three men looked at him as though they couldn't believe what their ears had taken in.

"But, jeez!" Shorty Wing exclaimed. "Why didn't you drop out of the game, when you saw the cards were running against you. We all did."

"Oh, you've played poker with Flecker, too, eh?" Jerry asked.

"Each of us have, but we had sense enough to pull out after losing a few pots."

"Now you know why you lost those pots," Jerry stated.

"Marked cards!" Hackett exclaimed bitterly. "Why that dirty, connivin' bustardly son of a lousy sheepherder—"

"Cripes, Jerry," Reed asked, "why did you stay in the game? A feller would figure you actually wanted to lose your cash."

"I already told you I'm sort of dumb," Jerry stated. "Incidentally, I want you three hombres to remember that. I'm so stupid I don't know which direction is up. That clear?"

The three eyed him narrowly. Finally Reed said, "I'll remember it, but I don't believe it. Dumb? Yeah, just like a fox, I figure. So you had to get a job some way, and that's the way you took to hook on with Flecker. What game you playing, Jerry?"

"I'm not ready to say yet," Jerry replied. "All

you three got to remember is that I'm sort of stupid."

"So now," Shorty Wing put in, "you're picked for the job all three of us refused, I'm bettin'."

"What job is that?" Jerry queried.

"Well, Flecker had some idea that we should ride out and pick up a few Two-M cows and deliver 'em—well, we never did learn where we was to herd 'em to, 'cause we all three refused on the grounds it wasn't accordin' to Hoyle."

"Oh." Jerry considered. "And then Flecker didn't dare tie the sack to you for fear you'd talk about what he wanted."

"That's the way it looked to us." Hackett nodded.

Jerry considered that too. He looked musingly off across the range where, beyond the low foothills, the San Lucia peaks etched rugged teeth against the western sky. It was nearing noontime now.

Shorty Wing said, "Well, it's 'bout time to go get a rise out of Cornpone Jones and tell him to fix us some sandwiches and coffee. He doesn't dast put a dinner on the table in the bunkhouse when Kelt is sleepin'. Kelt would skin him alive for disturbin' his slumber."

Then Jerry deposited another bomb. He said abruptly, "I thought a heap of Dennis Wolcott."

The other three stiffened, looking puzzled, staring at Knight.

Frank Reed asked, "You knew him?"

"Knew him well at one time."

"But—say, look here, Jerry—you asked a few minutes back if he was a range detective," Hackett stated. "Just like you'd never heard of him before."

Jerry smiled thinly, confessing, "That was just a feeler. I was trying to find out if you hombres knew anything special, or what folks thought of Wolcott around here."

"Yeah, dumb like a fox," Reed muttered.

"Oh," Hackett said after a moment. "Well, was he a Cattlemen's Association detective?"

"I don't think so."

"Well," Wing asked bluntly, "are you?"

"Am I what?" Jerry asked.

"Damn it"—Wing grinned—"you know what I mean. Are you working for the Association?"

Jerry smiled, looked Wing straight in the eyes. "Far from it, Shorty."

"Well, what—?" the other began, then paused. "Cripes! It ain't none of my business. Let it go. But in case you need any help doin' what you got in mind, I'm your man. C'mon, let's go talk Cornpone out of some chow."

"And then for me," Jerry observed, "my bunk. I'm beginning to feel in need of some shut-eye."

# VII

After he'd had a feed, accompanied by Cornpone Jones' half-drunken complaining, Jerry left his companions and sought his bunk. He noticed that Flecker, Corwin, Jacklin and Beadle were still sleeping soundly.

It must have been about six in the evening when a loud banging on a dishpan aroused the sleepers, with the call for supper. Jerry slipped from his bunk and went outside to wash in a tin washbasin that stood just outside the door. A considerably-soiled long towel hung there on a hanger; from a chain was suspended a comb with many of the teeth missing. Some way he managed to clean up with the supplies at hand and returned to the bunkhouse to find Flecker and the other three men, stretching, yawning and grumbling as they crawled from bunks. None of them said anything to Jerry.

Cornpone Jones appeared, toting a big box which contained tableware, plates, cups, and platters of beans and bacon. He deposited these on the table and left. Within a few minutes he returned with a couple loaves of sourdough bread and a big bowl of boiled potatoes. A third trip resulted in the delivery of a huge pot of black coffee and tins of condensed milk. Hackett, Wing and Reed sauntered in and found places at the table. Jerry noted that Cornpone wasn't quite steady on his feet.

Flecker and the others were already seated, waiting. Flecker swore at the cook. "Hereafter, Cornpone," he growled, "I want all the chow on the table, waitin', before you wake me up with that dishpan bangin'. I already told you that before, a couple of times."

"Sure 'nough, you did," the cook replied insolently, with a hiccough to punctuate the words. "I just keep fergittin'."

"You'll fergit once too often," Flecker snapped irritatedly. "And the Circle-F will have a new cookie herdin' your range. And you'll be gone—"

"That so?" Cornpone snarled. "Where you goin' to hire a new cook round here?" He faced Flecker defiantly. "I ain't heard of nobody cravin' this job on the Circle-F. Mebbe you ain't liked so well in Topango Wells, Kelt."

That stopped Flecker momentarily. He swore under his breath, then raised his voice angrily: "Cornpone, you been hittin' the bottle again. All day, every day, you jest sit and drink."

Cornpone uttered a cackling laugh. "You know anythin' better to do with whisky, Kelt?"

Flecker didn't answer that. He went on, "And furthermore I'm gettin' sick and tired of beans and bacon every night. Can't you rustle some steaks now and then?"

“Could be,” Cornpone retorted, “if—*hic!*—you’d butcher one of them strange brands I see you herdin’, round here, ever’ now and then—”

“Shut up!” Flecker roared. He half rose from the table, his features apoplectic. “Shut up and get out pronto, you hear? Don’t come in here again until you’re called for—and learn to keep your loud mouth shut, or it’ll be the worse for you.”

Again that cackling laugh from Cornpone, proving he wasn’t intimidated. “You’d best learn to mind your manners, Kelt,” he advised tartly, “or someday—*hic!*—you’ll find yourself cookin’ your own grub.” He was backing toward the doorway now, as he delivered his parting shot, “An’ furthermore—*hic!*—if you’d cut a doorway from this bunkhouse into my kitchen, I could get chow on the table faster. And I already told you that several times, but I reckon I ain’t the only one to forget—”

Flecker howled a string of profanity and, picking up his cup of hot coffee, hurled it after the already vanished cook, where it splashed against the edge of the doorjamb. No one else said anything, though Jerry could see several of the men suppressing smiles. Apparently, this sort of scene transpired every so often.

Flecker plopped down in his chair, cursing. Reaching across to Beadle’s place, which was next to his own, he seized Beadle’s cup of coffee, saying, “Go get yourself another cup, Tim.”

Beadle scowled, but didn’t say anything. Rising, he hurried out of the doorway, returning in a few minutes with another cup, which he proceeded to fill from the big pot. “His royal highness damn nigh took my head off, when I got this,” he complained.

“Damned if I wouldn’t hire a new cook, if I could find one,” Flecker growled. “Maybe I’ll have to break in one of you hands. Reed, you ever do any cookin’?”

Frank Reed stated he never had and didn’t intend to start. Flecker looked at the other men, but remained silent as he saw the same reply in their features.

Supper was finally concluded. Cornpone entered to clear away the dishes, albeit a trifle unsteadily. Flecker didn’t say anything to him, and the old cook remained silent.

Once the table was clear, Flecker tried to get another poker game started. “Ain’t nothing but some old cards here, but I got ’em from Hippo, so they’re all right.”

Jerry refused to rise to the bait, as did Reed, Wing and Hackett. Beadle, Corwin and Jacklin announced they were going to turn in early and catch up on some more “shut-eye.”

Flecker said nastily, “You lost your nerve, Knight? I’ll stake you—”

Jerry shook his head. “It’s not my nerve I’m

thinking about," he smiled thinly, "it's my independence I'm afraid of losing. I'm aiming to catch up on some more sleep, too."

Wing, Hackett and Reed commented that it had been right warm that afternoon and they intended to go out and enjoy the cool of the evening. Shortly afterward they left the bunkhouse.

"Goddamn soft crew I got ropin' for me," Flecker observed disgruntledly. "All's they think about is coolin' off and catchin' up on sleep."

"Could be," Jerry commented, "we're all not so tough as you, Kelt."

Flecker smiled sourly. "That's 'bout it."

The last thing Jerry remembered when he went back to his bunk was Flecker working over some papers at the end of the room which he called his office. He didn't know when the other men turned in.

The following morning after breakfast—the running feud between Flecker and Cornpone seemed to have reached another truce—Jerry went down to the corral to get his pony, and found Shorty Wing already there before him.

Shorty said, "I've been looking over that black gelding of yours, Jerry. Damn nice chunk of horse-flesh, but he looks a mite jaded."

"Could be," Jerry nodded. "He's come a long way, without much rest."

"Figured that," Wing said. "If you want to rest him another day or so, there's some good hosses here. You can take your pick. That chestnut with the white front legs is okay. Likewise, the paint hoss there, and that gray. That gray's a stayer, but ain't got much speed."

"Thanks, Shorty. That chestnut looks okay with me."

He entered the corral, carrying saddle and rope and cut out the horse, and then climbed into the saddle, sensing at once the chestnut was a prime animal.

Herb Jacklin had already saddled and loped out of sight beyond the first swell of range. The other hands were scattered about the buildings, somewhere, busy with various tasks.

Jerry found Flecker awaiting him in front of the bunkhouse. Here he dismounted again, saying cheerfully, "What's your orders, boss?"

"You bein' a stranger to this section of the range," Flecker commenced, "I've drawed you a map of the country hereabouts, so's you won't get lost. Here, take a look at this . . ."

Flecker produced a small black leather wallet from which he removed a white sheet of paper; on it was a crudely drawn, rough map of the surrounding terrain.

"Now you see here," Flecker began, while Jerry looked over his shoulder, "here's the San Lucia mountain range, directly west, running north and south. Here we are"—pointing to a dot on the map—"due east of the San Lucias. This is Circle-F holdin's. Now, if you head slightly southwest, you'll ford Aliso Creek, which runs a southeast course after headin' in the mountains. That creek is the boundary line between our outfit and Mark Monroe's Two-M spread; on the southwest. Monroe's outfit takes a sort of fish-hook curve and borders Circle-F property on the north for a way—"

Jerry interrupted. "You aren't going to tell me you're having boundary line trouble with Monroe's Two-M?"

"Hell, no! Nothin' like that. We're right friendly with the Two-M spread. They mind their business and we mind ours."

"That's good. I'd hate like poison to get mixed into any range wars in strange country."

"God A'mighty!" Flecker growled. "I ain't stinkin' mean enough to send a new hand into a mess of that kind—even was there such a mess, which same there ain't. I'll go even further than that. Should you see any strange riders around, light out as fast as you can. I aim to see you don't get in no trouble."

"If you're on good terms with the Two-M, where would any trouble be likely to come from?" Jerry asked, frowning slightly.

Flecker didn't reply at once. Finally, "Well, some of them fool hoe-men might get proddy. They seem to blame the Randall Company for all their hard luck. Just as if we could prevent

Aliso Creek from runnin' dry in hot weather."

"I understand." Jerry nodded.

Flecker continued quickly, "Now, here's what you do. Cross Aliso Creek—there'll be damn little water in it this time of year—then ride for the point where the creek corners into the foothills of the San Lucias—"

"But wouldn't that be getting awfully close to Two-M holdings?"

"Close, yes," Flecker said impatiently. "Look here, am I givin' instructions, or are you?"

"You are," Jerry said meekly. "Go on. Sorry I interrupted."

Flecker grunted scornfully. "You ride where I'm tellin' you to ride. Just about there, there's always a bunch of Two-M cows grazin'. They're prime stock and they never have no riders near 'em. You commencin' to get my point?"

Jerry's eyes narrowed. "Well, sort of, but maybe I'm kind of slow in my thinking. You said you were on friendly terms with the Two-M outfit."

"Hell's-bells! We are." Flecker chuckled. "But if Monroe is fool enough to leave his cattle unwatched, we'd be bigger fools to ride herd on 'em for him. All's you have to do is cut out about twenty-five of them prime beefs, and drive 'em over on our range. Then you head 'em for Camino Canyon—see, here's the canyon on this map. It's about eight-ten miles northeast of here.

Nice wide canyon, lots of good grass. You'll find somebody there to take the stock off'n your hands. Then you come home. That's all you got to do. Simple, eh?"

Inwardly, Jerry was seething with anger, but he continued his dumb act. "That don't seem exactly honest to me," he stated dubiously. "Stealing a friendly outfit's cows."

Flecker burst into a sudden guffaw that shook his bulky shoulders. "Sure, now, Knight, you don't figure we aimed to steal them cattle, did you? Shucks, boy, that's a right unkind thought. We just aim to take care of 'em for a spell."

"Yeah," Jerry objected, temper getting the better of him momentarily, "take care of 'em until you can run 'em over the county line, or maybe the Mexican border, forge a phony bill of sale and—"

"That's enough of that pious line," Flecker thundered, face clouded up like a thunderstorm. "Tell me it don't seem honest—hell! Buffalo chips on you! And your honesty. I don't understand, stupid as you are, how you got away with—"

"Well, I ain't going to do it," Jerry stated flatly.

"You're going to do it and like it," Flecker stated wrathfully. "Look here, Knight, I almost lost my temper. For a minute I had a good notion to plug you—"

"I happen to have a gun, too," Jerry said defiantly.

"Know how to use it, too, don't you?" Flecker sneered.

"I could try it." Jerry appeared to be cooling down.

"You'd be a fool to cross guns with me, Knight. I don't just try—*I do!*" Flecker held back his wrath a moment. "Look here, you'd best be reasonable. I'm sorry I lost my temper for a second. You and me are goin' to get along hunky-dory, if you'll just show some sense. I aim to convince you you're wrong."

"You're going to have a tough job doing that."

"Mebbe not, Knight. You just refused to follow instructions."

"I refused to turn cow-thief."

"Like that, eh?" Flecker sneered. "You forget you signed an agreement to work for me, take my orders? You tryin' to break that agreement, Knight?"

"I'm willing to do the work, honest work," Jerry said slowly, "but no honest man would expect me to do the work when you're giving crooked orders."

"You talk like a prime idiot," Flecker growled. "All that palaver 'bout honesty." He considered a moment, then: "Knight, how would you feel about goin' back to the penitentiary?"

Jerry stiffened. "Huh? What you hinting at?"

"I ain't hintin' and you know it. And don't try to pull that innocent trick on me. I'm wise to what you're up against."

"I'm waiting to hear," Jerry said coldly.

Flecker's lips widened in a nasty grin. "Don't try to bluff me, Knight. You ain't a good enough poker player to do that. I suppose you're going to claim that you're not out on parole, right now"—noting Jerry's sudden start of surprise, he went on—"and that you've already broken that parole by stepping out of the state that paroled you, after you'd only served three years of a ten-year stretch. I suppose that's news to you, eh?"

Knight fell silent. After a moment he swallowed hard and said in low tones, "That's right interesting information, Kelt. Where did you hear—?"

"Goddammit," Flecker swore. "I warned you not to try to run no bluff on me. I suspicioned you the minute I heard your name, the night you entered Hippodrome Casey's saloon. I recollected hearin' 'bout you before. There was a piece about you in the *El Paso Gazette* when you was paroled, six months back. I always manage to hold on to such clippin's, figurin' the hombre mentioned might come slopin' over to this range where mebbe I could make use of him. Want to see that clippin'?"

Flecker produced a small printed article, cut from newspaper stock, and held it, mockingly, before Knight's eyes. He read a few words: " 'Knight—better knowed as Jerry. Might be dangerous with a gun.' You was too dangerous for one hombre, once, wasn't you?"

Knight reached out one hand. "Let me see that clipping—"

Flecker jerked the paper out of reach. "No, you don't, killer. I'm keepin' this piece safe, case'n I have to show it to Deputy-Sheriff Buck Drake. But so long's as you do what I tell you, I'll keep my trap closed to Drake. You goin' to be fool enough to deny what this paper says, Knight?"

"Well," Knight said slowly, gathering his wits for the right words, "you might say there were mitigating circumstances that led to the shooting. Maybe that clipping tells about that, too—"

"Mitigatin' circumstances don't bring a dead man to life." Flecker chuckled in evil triumph. "You done your three years, then 'cause somebody offered you a job, the state authorities paroled you. Got off right easy, I'd say. Wouldn't you?"

Knight didn't say anything.

Flecker went on, "But what happened to that job? A condition of that parole was that you wasn't to leave the State of Texas. And here you are, clear over here in this territory. Can you explain that, cow-nurse?"

Knight showed a little spirit. "Could be I don't have to explain it."

"That's what you think. You'll explain plenty before I get through with you, Knight. You're a hell of a long way over the Texas line. That right?"

Knight's face worked angrily. "Admitted I've left Texas," he snapped, "so what about it?"

"That's what's got you in a hole, waddie." Flecker laughed confidently. "Sure, a man can get hisself out of a little scrap like jumpin' parole, if he plays his cards right—but I already proved you're no cardplayer. But holdin' up a stage, later, ain't no little scrape."

Knight studied the man's features. "What are you hinting at now, Flecker?"

"Me, I don't need to hint. I'm throwin' a straight rope, and you'd best take a look at it, and then think things over before you get proddy with Kelt Flecker. Hell! I've got the deadwood on you."

"I'm waiting to hear," Knight said.

"And I've got another piece from another newspaper to prove my point," Flecker half-snarled. " 'Tween the Texas line and here there's a lotta country, and on a lonely bend in the trail there was a stage holdup—'member? And you plugged the guard in the shoulder and made the driver throw down the strongbox, then told him to drive on, which same he did, wantin' to get his wounded guard to the doctor soon's possible—"

Knight's scornful laugh interrupted the words.

"You've been having a pipe dream, Flecker. I didn't have a thing to do—"

"Don't lie to me, Knight. You was just fool enough to look around when the stage pulled out, after you had the strongbox. And that bandanna slipped down off'n your face, and passengers in the coach got a good description of you—redheaded, same features, same build, practically the same togs you wore when you come into Hippo's place, night before last, with all that talk about havin' wages in your pocket. Wages from that strongbox, eh? Which same was found later with the lock shot off."

"I never had anything to do with any stage holdup," Knight muttered, though he wasn't meeting Flecker's gaze now.

"Don't lie to me, Knight. I've got you dead to rights, and my patience is growin' damn short. Make up your mind, road agent—do you want to go back to the pen with stage holdup added to your crime, or are you ready to follow my orders?"

Knight looked glum, downcast. Finally he drew a long sigh and started to climb back into his saddle. "Reckon I haven't got much choice in the matter," he stated heavily. "Guess I'll have to obey instructions."

Flecker laughed triumphantly. "Thought I could bring you to see reason, cowpoke. You be a right hombre and we'll all make money. Cross me, and you'll find yourself starin' at a window full of steel bars. And don't get any idea 'bout driftin' out of the country when you leave here. One word to Deputy Drake and you'll have a posse on your trail. . . . Oh, yes, Knight, be sure you pick out plump critters."

Knight gulped, started to turn the pony. Flecker said, "Here, don't forget to take this map with you. I wouldn't want you to get lost—now."

Replacing the map in the black wallet, he handed it up to Knight.

"I won't be needing that leather case, Kelt."

"Go on, take it. I don't want it. It's been kickin' around for the last year or so. You'll need that map a lot, 'fore we get through. That wallet will keep it from getting mussed, if you got a case to keep it in. I don't aim to be drawin' maps for dumb cowpokes every time I give 'em instructions. Now, get goin', Knight. I'll expect you back here a mite after suppertime, and if you ain't here, I'll be sendin' a man ridin' to spill a few things to Buck Drake."

Knight jerked his hat brim over his eyes, turned the pony and started off without a word.

Flecker snickered and called after him, "Don't go 'way mad. Ain't you even goin' to say good-bye?"

But Knight kept going without making a reply.

Grinning widely, Flecker reentered the bunk-house. George Corwin and Tim Beadle were sitting at the long table. They glanced up as Flecker came in.

Beadle asked, "Did the sucker take the bait?"

"Jesus!" Flecker said scornfully. "What else could he do? He didn't have no choice when he seen what I knowed about him."

"Bet he was plumb surprised," Corwin said.

"Downright flabbergasted," Flecker grunted. "I sure threw a scare into him. He'll toe the mark, until—well, you know what I mean. There's a slim chance he might get some Two-M cows and get 'em up to Camino Canyon, but I doubt that. Dumb as he is, he don't stand no chance buckin' the odds against him. He'll play straight with us, or he might get lost in a fog—a fog made by powder smoke. And if one plan don't work, there's a good chance ol' Mart Monroe might draw a bead on him. Boys, I figure our plan is airtight."

Flecker left the bunkhouse again, and found Frank Reed at one of the corrals.

Flecker asked Reed, "You had a chance to size up Knight yesterday, Reed. What'd you think of him?"

Reed hesitated, shrugged his shoulders. "It ain't for me to criticize any man you hire, Kelt."

"Forget that. I want an honest opinion."

"We-ell," Reed said slowly, "me'n Shorty and Steve figured him as mebbe bein' not too bright—a slow-thinker, sort of."

" 'Bout the way I sized him up, too." Flecker nodded. "On the other hand, I've had word he's a dangerous man with a gun."

"Possible," Reed conceded, "but that don't signify, neither. A hombre without brains can sometimes be dangerous if he gets a gun in his hand. A good gunfighter needs a hell of a lot of intelligence—"

"Which same Knight ain't got." Flecker smirked. "Not like me, for instance."

# VIII

Heading toward the southwest, Knight pushed the chestnut pony along at a brisk lope, until the first rise of land took him beyond sight of the Circle-F ranch buildings. Only then did he slow pace a trifle, his course bringing him nearer to the foothills of the San Lucia mountain range.

Certainly it was good grazing country hereabouts, with lush grass, dotted here and there with a clump of prickly pear cactus or an occasional mesquite tree with its fronds waving in the slight breeze lifting across the range. Now and then were to be seen outcroppings of a sort of reddish-brown granite, many of them reaching higher than a mounted man's head; a few were even larger, lifting their jagged outlines toward the sapphire sky, where but few clouds floated.

As the miles drifted behind him he soon found himself climbing and descending the first slopes of the San Lucia foothills. Now he was beginning to see Circle-F cows, grazing here and there in small bunches. Knowing cows never strayed too far from available water, Knight guessed he must be nearing Aliso Creek.

In this supposition he wasn't wrong. Fifteen minutes later he neared a line of low cottonwood trees, with here and there some alders, that lined either side of the creek. He pushed on and drew the chestnut to a splashing halt in the middle of a broad, shallow stream of clear water, which didn't reach quite to his stirrups. Glancing at the banks on either side, Jerry Knight could see that the stream was already running low as the hot weather settled in.

While the pony was swallowing long drafts of the cooling water, Jerry drew out the black wallet and studied the map Flecker had drawn for him. Now he had the terrain better fixed in his mind.

As he refolded the map and was about to replace it in the black leather case, a tiny glint of gold, little more than a speck, caught his eye on the black leather. Jerry frowned and scrutinized the wallet more closely, then understanding came to him.

At some time or other, a name, in gold lettering, had been stamped into the leather. Someone had gone to great pains to scratch out the gold in an effort to obliterate the name, but the imprint of the lettering stamp was still visible, even with the gold removed. An *e* showed quite plainly, as did a *c* and a *t*. Further close study brought out a capital *D* and a capital *W*.

"Mighty interesting," Jerry muttered. "Now, what the—?" He left the thought unspoken, raised his head and reined the chestnut out on the opposite bank of the stream. Checking the pony's tendency to continue moving, he thoughtfully rolled a brown paper Durham cigarette, lighted it and, exhaling gray smoke from his nostrils, gave his undivided attention to the faint letters on the black leather wallet. Not too faint at that; once brought to a man's attention, the stamping could be readily deciphered.

One by one the various letters revealed themselves to his eyes, until they had spelled out the name: Dennis Wolcott. Jerry scowled angrily now as certain things began to come more clearly to mind. For a brief moment he was shaken with anger, then cooled down again, as certain details began to dovetail into place.

"It's beginning to be plain as the sharp hammer mark on an exploded shell," Jerry told himself, tight-lipped. He gazed a moment, unseeing, across the range, as details began to drop into place. "Dennis Wolcott caught Ridge Conway in some skulduggery, and the two shot it out. Dennis killed Conway, but was, himself, wounded. Unbeknown to Dennis, Conway had a friend near, and killed Dennis by shooting him in the back. Just as Deputy Buck Drake has suspected, there was a third man in that deal. According to Wing, Reed and Hackett, Kelt Flecker and Ridge Conway had been close friends. Someone had stolen Dennis Wolcott's black leather wallet and then endeavored to remove the lettering. It was Flecker who gave Jerry the wallet. Was Kelt Flecker the third man in the case?

"Of course"—Jerry tried to be fair—"someone might have given that wallet to Flecker—maybe one of his other scouts. And that," he muttered grimly, "is something I aim to learn before I leave this range. The way things are shaping up, I may be able to leave a lot sooner than I planned—maybe on the end of a fast chunk of lead slug."

Replacing the map and wallet within his shirt, he touched spurs to his pony's ribs and cleared the trees on the opposite side of Aliso Creek, then took a more northerly course, though following the stream up to where it headed in the foothills. Here the grass grew luxuriantly, though tumbled heaps of large rock caused him to swerve course from time to time.

And then, quite suddenly, Jerry dipped down into a wide grassy hollow, across which were grazing about three hundred sleek, white-faced cattle, bearing on the left ribs the Two-M brand mark.

Jerry glanced quickly and cautiously around. Excepting himself there wasn't a rider of any kind in sight. Touching spurs to the chestnut he moved toward the nearest cows.

"Flecker said," he remembered, "to cut out twenty-five or thirty nice plump critters. Hell, they all look to be in prime shape." He muttered resentfully as his thoughts took form. "Flecker's just wastin' breath with that line and he's one damn fool if he figures I'm going to bother choosing what I take. I'll cut from the bunch nearest me and then fantail out of this neighborhood as fast as I can drive the critters. I don't reckon it would be very healthy was I to be caught, red-handed, stealing another man's cows, right out of his backyard, you might say."

He uncoiled his rope and, using it to startle the animals into motion, started toward the nearest cattle. For ten minutes he worked strenuously, cutting out some twenty animals from the others. His shirt was streaked with sweat; beads of perspiration dotted his features, so intent was he on working quickly and then leaving, with the cows, as soon as possible.

And then it happened!

Jerry was just reining his pony around a tall upthrust of rock in pursuit of an obstreperous cow, that kept trying to dodge back, when a leaden slug *spat-flattened* itself against the rock with a sort of silvery splash. Almost instantly the report of a rifle reached Jerry's ears!

With one smooth motion, Jerry jerked the pony to a halt, whirling in the saddle as he spun the horse around to face the unseen shooter. There was nobody to be seen. In front of Knight were only rocks and waving grass.

Crouching low in the saddle, one fist clenched about the butt of his six-shooter, eyes darting swiftly here and there, Jerry endeavored to catch sight of the hidden rifleman. But nowhere could he spot any motion indicating the presence of a man.

Knight raised his voice: "Show yourself, hombre, if you want another chance. That shot was right close, but if you want a second try, you got to put in an appearance."

This was largely bluff, as Jerry realized, but he'd hoped to scare the hidden assailant into view. But the bluff failed to work. Even as he'd spoken, Jerry was realizing that picking up cows on another owner's range was enough to damn him, and while he had his gun ready, he was uncertain in his mind whether he'd use it. Already a guilty flush was mounting to his face.

Tensely, Jerry awaited a reply, wondering when it came whether it would arrive verbally or in the form of a leaden missile. The answer, when it did come, surprised him, consisting, as it did, of a single scornful laugh, and from a point much nearer Jerry and in a slightly different direction than he had expected.

He moved his gaze toward a high, wide granite outcropping—nearly the size of a small house—from behind which the laugh had sounded.

And now Jerry saw the end of the rifle barrel pointing at him, and the figure behind the gun. The figure spoke contemptuously:

"Drop that gun on the ground. Quick! I'm holding a bead on you, cow-thief, so move pronto!" As Jerry's six-shooter thudded to earth, the voice continued, "Now, raise 'em high, and don't waste any time about it. Quick!"

There was nothing else for Jerry to do. He raised his hands above his head, then lowered them slightly to clasp his hands across the crown of his sombrero.

"Now do you dare to come into view?" he challenged coolly. "Or are you afraid to move out of that shadow?"

Again that scornful laugh, and the rider moved into sunlight, though she was dismounted now and leading her horse behind her. Jerry had already suspected the truth when he'd heard her voice. But the rifle was still at ready, cradled in one arm.

Jerry forced a laugh. "The disgrace of it," he groaned, "to be captured by a woman. I figured it might be a woman when that shot missed—"

The girl's voice blazed. "I can shoot as straight as any man," she flared hotly.

"I'm not saying you can't," he said coolly. "A man wouldn't have missed at that distance."

"I missed you on purpose," the girl snapped.

" 'Course you did. That's the point I'm making. Women being such tenderhearted creatures don't like to kill—"

"Cut the sweet-talk, rustler man," the girl cut him short. "It doesn't make any time with me. Jiminey! I could have bored you plumb center."

"I'm still wondering why you didn't," he said mildly.

"I'm a fool," the girl said bitterly. "It's just your good luck it wasn't Dad or one of the hands throwing down on you, or you'd be done, thief—"

"And on my way to Heaven," Jerry finished. "Glad you didn't kill me. I never could learn to play a harp and wear wings."

"More likely you'd be learning to shovel coal, where you'd go." The girl's lips twitched a little. "You're a cool one, I must say."

Jerry shrugged. "No use my getting hot under the collar. I know when I'm licked. So—what happens now?"

"That's up to Dad and the boys." The girl spoke tartly. "I'm taking you prisoner—stop! What do you think you're doing?"

Jerry had thrown one leg over his saddle, and stepped to the ground.

The girl edged around to get a full view of him. "You reach for your gun there and you're a goner," she warned coldly. "What are you up to?"

"Just getting down from my saddle," Jerry explained. "I was always taught not to remain seated when a lady is standing. Now if you will sit down, maybe we can both take a load off our boots."

The girl studied him in some perplexity. "Say, exactly what sort of a nut are you?"

"What kind of nuts do you like?"

Jerry was grinning inwardly at her puzzled manner. She was really a very pretty girl, with great masses of blue-black hair coiled beneath her well-weathered gray sombrero. Her dark eyes displayed unbelievably long lashes. Red lips and a somewhat wide mouth, above a determined chin. Rather high cheekbones. All her curves seemed to be in the right places. She wore a man's blue denim shirt, rolled to the elbows and displaying well-tanned, rounded arms. She wore a man's blue Levi's and a somewhat scuffed pair of high-heeled riding boots. The horse she sat was a wiry gray.

"All's I've got to say," Jerry went on, "if I had to be captured, I've got to admit I'm enjoying it."

"How you figuring that?" the girl asked curiously.

"There's nothing like being taken in by a beautiful woman," Jerry replied.

"Thanks for the compliment, but I already warned you I wasn't to be taken in by any sweet-talking." The girl hesitated a moment, then added, "Dirty, slippery cow-thief," in contemptuous tones.

"Them's harsh words, ma'am," Jerry stated reprovingly.

"Well, aren't you? I've been watching you quite a spell. You can't deny I saw you cutting out our cows. I saw you were a stranger and I hesitated to shoot on that account—the more fool I'm proving to be. Dad wouldn't have let you off that easy. We've lost all too many cows the past year, and Dad's about at the end of his patience. You can't deny you're a cow-thief, can you?"

Jerry didn't reply, just stood gazing admiringly at the girl.

A slow flush crept into her face, as she sensed his admiration. Her lips tightened suddenly. "Well, answer me! Aren't you a cow-thief?"

Jerry shrugged. "I'll admit appearances are against me, but you shouldn't always judge by appearances, ma'am."

The girl studied him. Despite herself, her reasoning against such thought, she found herself liking this stranger. There was a chance he had made a mistake in cutting out Two-M cows. She decided to give him a chance to explain his actions.

She frowned a little, uncertain what to do. Certainly, he had kept cool under fire. Her shot didn't seem to have shaken him in any way. Under the circumstances, she couldn't quite comprehend his levity, and she had to admit he hadn't acted, at all, like a cow-thief, apprehended in stealing cows.

Still, she hesitated. Finally she said, level-voiced, "*Phoo!* Appearances! How else was I to judge your actions?"

"You fired without even giving me a chance to

explain. A mite quick with your trigger-finger, weren't you?"

Her frown deepened a little. "You claiming you aren't really a cow-thief? That you have a plausible excuse for your actions?"

"Yes, ma'am." Jerry grinned. "You see, I was only following my foreman's orders."

"And he told you to steal our cows?"

"We-ell, I don't remember him using that word 'steal.' He simply said he was going to take care of your cows for a spell, and he sent me over here to get 'em. It's just that simple."

"It's not simple, at all," the girl snapped. She found herself growing angry again. "You look like a cowman. I watched you handling those cows. You seem to know your business. But you don't seem to understand what stealing means. What sort of talk—?" She broke off, then, "Say, cowboy, are you crazy?"

"Just a mite batty, I expect," he said humbly. "Maybe it's the view has sort of made me weak in the head."

"The view?"

"Uh-huh. And a sudden idea that seems to have overtaken me. That's it—the view. You know, the scenery. I can't remember when my eyes have been treated to such a beautiful sight. And then I got that idea. I thought, 'Gosh! It'd be wonderful to be married to such scenery.' And the whole idea sort of made my head swim—"

"Stop it!" Her rifle barrel lifted a trifle, as her cheeks abruptly crimsoned. "I warned you I didn't want to hear any soft soap palaver. As I see it, you're just plain insane."

"Yes'm. I agree. I don't ever expect to be the same again. But we've got to get better acquainted. My name's Knight. Folks close to me always call me Jerry. Do you think you could learn to say Jerry?"

"Now, just you cut out that sort of talk, *Mister* Knight." The girl's cheeks were still flushed. She tried to make her voice sound stern, but it wouldn't quite come off. She had to bite her lip to keep from laughing.

"Yep"—Jerry nodded imperturbably, as he continued—"nice dimples, too. Why don't you just go ahead and laugh right out loud? And you can make it *Mister* Knight, if you like, at present, but I reckon we'll have to put my full name on the license—"

"What in Heaven's name are you talking about? You can't get a license to steal cows—"

"Never wanted one. It's a wedding license I'm referring to. You and me. Say, I've got ten bucks that says your name's Samantha."

"I don't bet on sure things. You're wrong."

"Then it's Hepsabeth Minerva Abigail, or I'm a liar."

"You are. The name is Alice—Alice Monroe—"

"And a right pretty name that is," Jerry stated

promptly. "You see, I had to find out somehow, so I misnamed you a-purpose. Yep, you and me will get along fine, Alice, once we've come to an understanding—"

"*Miss* Monroe, to you," the girl said shortly. "And we're going to come to an understanding a lot quicker than you expect. Get on your horse, mister, and ride slow in front of me. We're headed for the Two-M. Dad will settle your hash—"

"That'll be our second misunderstanding. I never did care much for hash, so in the future—"

"Better mention that *first* misunderstanding, right now," snapped the girl, "and then straddle your pony."

Jerry made no move to obey, saying instead, "I can't, Alice. I got to do what my boss told me to do. I don't think he'd like it if I didn't bring some of your cows for him to take care of."

"Exactly who is your boss?"

"Man named Kelt Flecker—foreman of the Circle-F."

The girl's lip curled disdainfully. "That low-down coyote. I might have known—"

"Aren't you sort of hard on the whole coyote family, Alice?"

Her dark eyes narrowed. She scarcely knew what to make of this stranger she'd captured. "I suppose I am, at that," she conceded coldly. "And just remember, Mister Man, I'm *Miss* Monroe to you."

"Yes, Alice," he said meekly. "I'll try."

This time she let it pass, with only a helpless shake of the head and a tightening of the lips. "At least, in their way, most coyotes have a certain intelligence."

"Don't you think that same applies to Flecker?"

Alice Monroe gave a contemptuous shake of her head. "If Kelt Flecker had brains, he wouldn't send anybody as thickheaded as you to rustle our Two-M cows."

Jerry uttered a pained, "Ouch! Go easy with that needle, Doc."

The girl snapped, "If you're not entirely stupid, I can't see why you ever went to work for him. More and more you appear like something the cat dragged home. How in the world he ever came to hire you is more than I can understand—"

"He didn't come to hire me. I come to him."

"And you needed a job real bad, I suppose."

"No'm," Jerry explained humbly. "Yeah, I wanted the job all right, but I don't draw any wages—"

"No wages!"

"That's right. Flecker won me in a poker game."

The girl stared at him, eyes wide. "My good grief! In a poker game?"

"Want to hear how come?"

She hesitated, then nodded. "I'm just curious enough to listen to more of your silly talk—"

"Let's sit down then and I'll tell you about it."

The girl shook her head. "You just want to get nearer that six-shooter on the ground."

Jerry said impatiently, "Oh, cripes, don't be so suspicious. I trust you. Why can't you trust me? Here"—before the girl could lift her rifle, he stooped, retrieved the Colt's gun and tossed it at her feet. "Now you got both guns," he said, dropping to a sitting position on the grass. "Have a seat, Alice."

Warily, the girl settled to a position, cradling her knees in her arms, a few feet away from him and near his gun. The rifle was handy at her side. "You'd best make this mighty interesting, Mister Man—"

"The name's Jerry—remember?" He began: "It happened when we were holed up in Hippodrome Casey's saloon, the night the Topango Howler hit town. So there was this poker game and Flecker was demonstrating something I already knew—that three of a kind beats two pair. . . ."

From that point on, Jerry continued and related in full detail all the happenings that had occurred during the all-night poker session, resulting finally in his signing an agreement to work two months without wages for the Circle-F outfit.

The girl listened with increasing amazement as the tale was unfolded, believing Knight in spite of herself, and at the same time finding herself liking this strange cowpuncher. When he had concluded, she said caustically, "Cowboy, sometimes you don't sound too bright."

Jerry grinned. "That's what Kelt Flecker thinks, too."

She studied him a moment, admiring something she detected in his face. Some of the acid left her voice. "Well, Great Hannah! that certainly beats me."

"His poker hand beat me, too."

"But, Jerry, just because you signed a paper to follow orders doesn't mean you have to turn cow-thief. You could have dismissed that agreement, after you learned you were playing with marked cards. Can't you realize that?"

He nodded. "But look at the good luck it's brought me. Right now I'm kicking myself for not inspecting this neck of the range long ago."

"You find this interesting?"

"*She* sure is."

The girl flushed under his admiring survey. "We'll talk about the business at hand," she reminded him, trying to keep her voice chilly and not quite succeeding. "Seeing you're such a fool, I've decided to let you go. Maybe you've learned your lesson—"

"Suppose I don't want to be released. I like being your captive. Y'know, you should be fair and consider my feelings in the matter."

Alice Monroe threw up one hand in a helpless gesture. "I can see it's wasted time trying to talk sensibly to you," she stated emphatically. "I'm trying to talk on a common-sense basis and you—"

He broke in, "All right. I'll behave. What do you want me to do?"

"I want you to pick up your gun and ride back to the Circle-F as fast as your horse will carry you. What you do then is no concern of mine. Just get out of here—fast!"

"We won't argue that point right now," Jerry said dryly. "What are *you* intending to do?"

"I'm going to ride back home *muy* pronto and tell Dad about you, and tell him all the things you've told me. It's exactly the proof we need to stop Flecker. We've suspected him, but could never get proof. And then Dad will get Buck Drake on the job—"

"I wouldn't, was I you," Jerry interrupted. "You wouldn't get any place. Flecker would deny he ever sent me here. I'm a stranger here, and it would be Flecker's word against a stranger's. You'd have tipped your hand, given your plans away. And you'd spoil things for me—"

"What would we spoil for you?" she demanded.

"I've got to return with twenty or twenty-five cows," he evaded. Before she could insert an objection, he asked, "Have you been missing many cows lately?"

"Dad figures around two hundred head over the past year. We really should keep a man posted here every day, but we've a mighty big territory to cover and haven't enough hands. I just rode down here today to sort of look around. Dad has already sent out a warning stating any rustler he caught on his holdings would be shot on sight. Everybody in the San Lucia country knows that—including Kelt Flecker. He should have told you."

Jerry's eyes narrowed. "Could be he purposely withheld the information."

"You mean"—the girl sounded outraged—"Flecker wanted you to be killed?"

"It's possible." Jerry nodded slowly. "Dennis Wolcott was killed by an unknown over in this section, I understand."

"You know about that?" the girl asked in surprise. Jerry nodded. Alice went on, "I'll tell you something else. It's suspected in some quarters that Kelt Flecker is that unknown, but Buck Drake has never been able to prove it. He's still trying to run down that third man."

"Could be," Jerry mused, half-aloud, "that I'd make a prime suspect. You see, if you or one of your men had killed me, and a wallet of Dennis Wolcott's was found on my body—"

"Have you something of Wolcott's?"

"A black leather wallet that Flecker gave me." He added certain details.

The girl spoke angrily. "It certainly looks as though Flecker was trying to get rid of certain evidence that would make you look guilty."

"A nice bit of framing." He nodded coolly. "But if I'm in the picture, I'm not aiming to be hung."

"That settles it," the girl said decisively. "Buck Drake has certainly got to be told what we know."

Jerry shook his head. "Not yet. Before we spill any beans I want to know a few more things about this range."

Alice Monroe eyed him speculatively. "You aren't a Cattlemen's Association detective, are you?" she asked seriously.

Jerry laughed and shook his head. "Not none, lady. Matter of fact, if I told you who I really am, you'd just laugh at me, and tell me I should have a padded cell in the booby hatch. I doubt you'd even believe me."

"Well, from what I've heard so far, you couldn't blame me if I think you're a bit touched in the head."

She looked puzzled, but didn't press the questioning that rose in her mind. Finally, she came to a decision. "All right, I *think* you've spoken the truth, even though it does make you look witless. I won't say anything for a time—to Deputy Drake. But I am going to tell Dad when I get back home. Now, you'd better pick up your gun and ride."

Jerry nodded. "But please tell your Dad to keep his lip buttoned for a time."

Alice looked dubious. "I'll do what I can,

but my father has a habit of suiting himself on problems, regardless what I say."

Jerry nodded and, reaching over, retrieved his six-shooter. It was that move that doubtless saved his life: as he shifted position, there came a sharp whining sound past his ear, and a leaden slug snarled dangerously close to his head.

Almost simultaneously, from the hillside at their backs, came the sharp report of a Winchester rifle!

# IX

Even as he came to his feet, Jerry pushed the girl flat on the ground, with a terse, "Stay down!" then whirled and, gathering reins, vaulted into his saddle, swinging the pony in a sharp turn that almost swept the beast from its feet. Digging in his spurs, he lined out for the hillside, to where the shot from the hidden assailant had been fired.

He heard Alice's voice call after him, "Who is it?"

"That's what I aim to find out," he yelled back over one shoulder. "Now you stay down!"

The wind whipped viciously into his face as he rode fast up the gradual incline. Again, a rifle bullet kicked up dirt and dust just in front of his pony's feet, but Jerry was traveling too fast to make a good target, as he pushed ahead, crouched low in the saddle. From this position he peered up at the hillside, which was covered with thick brush, cactus and mesquite trees. There wasn't a soul to be seen. Then, he caught a sudden puff of gray smoke as the hidden rifleman fired a third time, the shot flying high over Jerry's head.

From behind, Jerry caught the sound of a series of fast rifle shots, as Alice started spraying the hillside with hot lead.

"Good girl," Jerry muttered. "She's trying to

cover my advance, but she should have stayed down, like I told her."

He pushed furiously, on, the way growing steeper. Then it became necessary to slow the pony as he found himself forced to thread a slower course through trees and brush. He was three-quarters of the way to the top of the hill now.

Apparently, the girl's firing had been effective, as the hidden man's firing had ceased. But where in the devil was he hiding out?

The trees and brush were higher here, and Jerry found himself forcing his way through a thicket of leafy shadows. Jerry pulled the horse to a halt and slipped down from the saddle. He stood there a moment, listening. The only sounds that reached his ears were the chirping of birds and the buzzing of insects.

Five minutes passed, then ten, while Jerry waited for the first indication of a movement on the part of his adversary. Once, he glanced down the long hillside, where the girl, standing now, warm sun beating on her uplifted face, held her rifle in a ready position.

Could Jerry have made out her features, he'd have seen the anxious look on her face as she waited as tensely as he, watching for some sign of him or the unknown gunman. Now, she didn't dare do any firing, for fear of hitting Jerry, hidden among the trees and brush.

The minutes dragged along. Her heart was beating madly, though she wasn't conscious of it at the moment. There were no more sounds to be heard on that hillside either, until—

Abruptly, a shot sounded through the hot stillness of the hillside. A few minutes later there came a second shot. Then two more in quick succession. Small clouds of black powder smoke rose above the greenery of the brush and trees.

Alice choked back the cry that rose to her lips, her eyes wide on the otherwise motionless hillside.

Meanwhile, Jerry had left his horse behind and went forward on foot, eyes scanning the underbrush in all directions, as he peered sharply about. From time to time some scrub oak and a few cottonwoods barred his way, at the same moment giving him a certain protection as he moved, through a veritable jungle of cactus and tangled spiny brush.

Suddenly, from Jerry's left, a shot roared. This time, from a six-shooter, carrying the thundering detonation of a forty-five caliber.

Though the shot flew wide of its mark, Jerry gave a sharp cry and dropped heavily to the earth. Rolling over and over, he soon screened himself behind a tall clump of brush and waited for the next move.

Silence. From overhead, spots of sunlight

pierced the thicket. Insects droned unceasingly in the silence, though now the birds had quieted. A minute passed and stretched out to five, while Jerry waited, alert for the first movement of his adversary.

Almost without warning there came the crunching of dry leaves beneath booted feet. More silence. Then that crunching, rustling sound again. A small branch snapped loudly in the stillness.

Then, a few yards away, peering to right and left, six-shooter raised to fire, came Herb Jacklin, his evil mind intent on locating and finishing the job he had commenced.

Jacklin tensed suddenly, as through the tangled thicket, he caught a brief glance of Jerry's riderless horse, a short distance off. Now he was facing partly away from Jerry's position.

Jerry rose to his full height. "Looking for a lost dog or something, Jacklin?" he asked coolly.

Jacklin swore a vicious oath and swung around to face the point from which Jerry's voice had issued. His gun-hand swung in a swift arc, but he was too unsettled by the surprise to fire with accuracy.

Jerry had jerked sidewise as Jacklin threw down on him, then triggered a swift shot from his own forty-four Colt gun.

Jacklin was swung half around by the impact of the tearing lead slug, then righted himself, started a scornful laugh that turned into a wracking cough.

As he tried to steady his six-shooter for another shot, Jerry's second bullet struck, sending a tiny puff of dust from the man's opened vest.

Then Jacklin's body jackknifed as he pitched forward on his face, crushing a small opuntia cactus beneath his body as he fell.

The man was already dead by the time Jerry reached him and turned him over. Blood was staining his shirt in two widening circles, placed quite closely together.

Gunsmoke fog was drifting lazily through the sunlight-spotted shadows. A breeze filtered through the brush, dissipating the last remnants of swirling gray haze. Jerry straightened from the body. His face was set in hard, grim lines.

He muttered to himself, "Well, there's one to square Dennis Wolcott's account—but it's going to take more than one, I figure."

He gazed a moment at the still motionless form, considered, rolled a cigarette and lighted it. His fingers were very steady. Then he punched out the empty shells in his gun cylinder, catching them in his hand and pocketing them, before reloading the depleted chambers.

His mind reverted to the girl, and he called loudly, hoping his voice would carry that far, "I'll be back in a few minutes, Alice." He was too far away to hear the girl's relieved exclamation.

Next, Jerry searched for Jacklin's horse and found it a short distance off, nibbling at a leafy mesquite branch. Gathering the reins, dragging on the earth, he tossed them back over the saddle, struck the animal a solid wallop on the rump and started it off, knowing eventually it would probably head for the Circle-F Ranch.

Then he found his own pony, mounted and made his way quickly down the hillside, breaking into a lope when he reached level ground.

The girl was already mounted when he reached her side. She studied his face gravely a moment before asking, "Well?"

He said, "Thanks for covering me when I was heading for that hillside. You probably saved me a heap of trouble—"

"It was nothing," she replied. "I was just shooting blindly hoping to—"

"Oh, we'd work well together in harness," he assured her. "I've been trying to tell—"

She interrupted, "You know, I do have a certain curiosity."

Jerry said quietly, "Lot of skunks in these hills, I reckon."

"But what happened?"

"There's one less skunk to plague the range," he said, sober-voiced.

The girl winced a little, glanced quickly over him to learn if he had been wounded, then, "Who was it?"

He evaded that. "You tell your dad about this. Better have him come out here and look things over. He'll know what to do. The deputy will have to be informed, of course. You might tell your dad to not be too ready to tell who's responsible. Right now I don't want to be called in to serve at an inquest—or maybe arrested. Your dad can just say a body has been found—"

The girl nodded. "I'll tell him, but he'll make up his own mind."

Jerry nodded. "You'd better spur your pony for home now. But first, I'd like to get the lay of the land here. Exactly who is Bristol Capron—that is, what do *you* know about him?"

"He's manager of the Randall Land & Cattle Company, owned by some man named Ira Randall who lives back East, someplace. As to Capron, a slimier reptile never lived, in my opinion. I don't trust him."

"The company apparently put him on the job."

"He's a fit man for such a company."

Jerry eyed her curiously. "What have you got against the Randall Company as a whole?"

"They're thieves! Land-hogs, cattle-hogs. They're trying to gobble up every bit of wealth in sight. I tell you, Ira Randall wouldn't dare show his face in this neck of the range." Her voice was bitter. "He'd be lynched on sight, I'm betting. The country hates him worse than poison. He's smart to stay in the East. But he sends Capron out to handle the dirty work."

"Could be you're wronging Randall, maybe," Jerry pointed out.

"If so, you'll have to show me where," the girl flamed. "His company issues mortgages to poor farmers, hoe-men, who can't possibly pay them off. Then they get foreclosed. After that the land is advertised and more farmers are found to take the bait. The Randall outfit is nothing but a greedy, merciless octopus. Why do you think Flecker is stealing our cattle?"

"I'm waiting to hear."

"So Dad will go broke and have to give up the Two-M. Capron has already made several offers for our ranch, but the amount he offers is so small Dad won't even listen to him."

"The Randall Company hold a mortgage on the Two-M?"

"No. Thank Heaven for that. So Capron wants to ruin us so he can get control."

"Any particular reason he wants your outfit in particular?"

"Plenty," Alice snapped. "Palo Verde Pass."

"You'll have to explain that."

The girl nodded. "Palo Verde Pass cuts through the San Lucias about six miles southeast of our ranch house. It's part of our holdings. The T.N. & A.S. Railroad would like the pass to extend its line from Topango Wells to farther west."

"Seems to me," Jerry said thoughtfully, "your dad would be wise to sell the railroad a right-of-way through the Pass. He could make some money and—"

"You don't understand," Alice cut in. "You see, right near the mouth of the Pass there's a nice stretch of tableland that overlooks the whole valley. Before my mother died, she and Dad had always planned to build a house there." The girl broke off, eyes slightly moist.

Jerry waited. Then the girl continued: "Someday I'd like to build a house there myself. This is pretty country. I wouldn't want that place spoiled by coal smoke and cinders and a lot of steel rails. We wouldn't want a lot of money. Only enough to get along comfortably. If the Randall Company would only leave us alone—"

Jerry said gently, "I can see your point, Alice. But folks the other side of the San Lucia Mountains would like railroad service, too."

"There's Camino Canyon, then," the girl flared. "It really wouldn't make much difference to the railroad. As a matter of fact, I think the T.N. & A.S. might sooner have it. Once through the pass, the ground levels off and—"

"Why doesn't the railroad buy a right-of-way through Camino Canyon then—that's not so far from the Circle-F ranch house, and is already on Circle-F holdings—"

"Because the Randall Company is holding out

for a terribly prohibitive price, and the railroad refuses to stand still for a holdup, and I can't blame it. If Bristol Capron could get control of the Two-M he'd ask similar money for Palo Verde Pass. And the railroad would eventually have to pay—holdup or not."

"I see." Jerry fell silent for a moment, then, "You'd best be sloping for home now. Tell your dad what's happened. Also, tell him not to bother counting his cows tomorrow, 'cause he's going to be about twenty cows short."

The girl had started to turn her horse. Now she checked it. "Now, look here, cowboy—" she bridled.

"Shucks"—Jerry grinned—"I've got to carry out the boss's orders. Now, wait a minute. Don't go to flying off the handle that way. I know what I'm doing."

"I wonder if you do," Alice said tersely. She looked slightly bewildered.

"You can bet your Stet hat on that. You may lose a few cows, but you stand to win in the long run. Take my word for it."

"We-ell—" The girl hesitated. "It sounds crazy, but—but—"

"But you'll let me leave with the cows and not shoot at me anymore? Fine! Now we're getting along right well, Alice. But you ain't seen nothing yet. I got plans—"

"What kind of plans?"

"Remember what I said about a license?"

The girl's face crimsoned. With a short ejaculation she spun the horse around and, using spurs, moved rapidly into a swift lope.

"I've got other plans too," Jerry yelled after her. "Leastwise, I'll have a good architect draw some—for a house on that nice tableland you mentioned."

The girl kept going with no answer.

Jerry raised his voice again. "Hey, I figure to be back day after tomorrow, after more cows. You'll be here, won't you?"

The girl turned in the saddle. "You couldn't stop me, now, cowboy"—and she was laughing—"and I'll have Dad with me, if not the whole Two-M crew. They'll all be curious to see what an escaped lunatic looks like."

She touched spurs to the horse and the animal bore her swiftly away, skirting widely the hillside where the dead Jacklin lay.

Jerry turned the chestnut and began cutting out cows again. Within a short time he had gathered some twenty-one head. Then, driving them before him, he started in the direction of the Circle-F.

# X

It was nearly four o'clock in the afternoon, when Jerry arrived near the Circle-F Ranch buildings, driving before him twenty-one head of Two-M beef cattle. Here he drew his pony to a halt, waiting.

"Now, watch Flecker hit the ceiling," he mused, somewhat humorously. "He's going to be mad as a tailed-up steer when he sees I brought these critters here."

And mad Flecker was! Flecker had already spotted him, and his angry bellow could be heard for miles, Jerry figured. The Circle-F foreman came striding wrathfully around the corner of a barn, violent oaths spewing from his lips.

"What in the devil you bringin' them animals here for?" he demanded hotly. "I told you plain to deliver 'em at Camino Canyon. By God! You ain't got sense enough to tell black from white. What in hell do you mean—?"

Jerry sat his saddle, coolly rolling and lighting a Durham cigarette, gazing down at Flecker and waiting for the man to run out of breath and end the tirade.

There finally came a pause in Flecker's outburst, and Jerry took advantage of the momentary quiet to say mildly, "Look, Bossman, I've done the best I could. I've brought you twenty-one head of prime beef, as you ordered—"

"But you should have delivered 'em to Camino Canyon," Flecker insisted hotly. "Can't you remember—?"

"Sure. I remember what you said." Jerry nodded. "But you got to remember something too. This range is strange to me. I was afraid it would get dark before I could locate the canyon. And remember, too, I ain't had any dinner, and it's getting nigh supper time—"

A bellow of rage broke from Flecker. "You makin' a god of your belly?" he wanted to know. "You can eat any time. When I give an order, I want it followed—"

"Look here, Kelt," Jerry offered placatingly, "you're just lucky I got any cows at all. There was two riders ridin' herd on those cows over there—"

"There was?" Flecker looked startled. "They never used to keep a watch on 'em."

"Well, there was today. Maybe they don't watch 'em close, though, 'cause after a spell they pulled out. But I had to keep hid behind a big rock for two-three hours until they left and I could cut out these cows. Like I say, I've done the best I know how."

Flecker frowned. He seemed a bit upset by the news. "Never knew 'em to have riders at that spot before," he growled.

"Well, they were there today."

"All right, Knight." Flecker seemed somewhat mollified. "You showed you had guts anyway, maybe, gettin' these critters when you knowed riders were so near. Could be you'll learn to be a top hand on the Circle-F in time."

"Thanks, boss," Jerry said dryly.

Struck by a new thought, Flecker asked in a rather offhand manner, "Say, you didn't happen to see Herb Jacklin over that way, today, did you?"

Jerry assumed a surprised look. "Did you send Jacklin to pick up some Two-M cows too?" he asked.

Flecker shook his head, and evaded, "No, it was a sort of different job I sent him ridin' on—somethin' that needn't concern you, Knight."

"Well, if he had seen me, don't you think he would have hailed me, or something?" A sudden irritated look swept across Jerry's face. "Look here, Kelt, you didn't send him over there to keep cases on me, did you? I wouldn't like that. If you can't trust me, how in hell do you expect—?"

"Take it easy, Knight, take it easy," Flecker interrupted in an appeasing tone. "I wouldn't pull no stunt like that on you. No, it was something else Jacklin was doing for me. I wonder if he got his orders mixed up and headed down for the Mexican border. I'd mentioned a few days ago I had some business down there for him to check for me—"

"Oh, maybe that was it." Jerry nodded.

Another idea suddenly occurred to Flecker. He muttered, half to himself, "If there was two Two-M riders over that way . . ." He was beginning to look a trifle concerned now. "Look here, Knight, when you were over that way, you didn't hear any gunshots, did you, or pick up any sign there'd been a fracas of any sort?"

Jerry laughed shortly. "Don't you think that would have been the first thing I told you about when I arrived?" he asked.

Flecker nodded. "Yeah, I reckon so. Damn funny Jacklin hasn't come back, though. I wonder what happened to him."

"You'll probably hear in time," Jerry said casually. "What do you want done with these cows? They're startin' to mill uneasy like and—"

"What?" Flecker seemed to be lost in thought. His brow looked troubled. Jerry repeated his question. Flecker replied in a growl, "We'll just have to keep 'em here overnight. You can deliver 'em at Camino Canyon tomorrow."

Shorty Wing had come sauntering up. He stood looking at the cows a moment, then offered Jerry a cool nod. Jerry said, "Hello, Shorty."

Wing was studying Jerry, looking somewhat disappointed. He couldn't quite figure out why

Knight had fallen in with Flecker's plan to steal Two-M cows.

"Wing," Flecker asked, "you didn't hear Herb Jacklin mention where he was ridin' when he left this mornin', did you?"

Wing shook his head. "He didn't say anything in my hearin'."

Flecker shook his head, puzzledly, then said, "Wing, get Reed or Hackett and head these cows into that empty corral down at the end there."

"There's some bars missin' in that old corral," Wing started to point out.

"Well, goddammit, fix 'em," Flecker roared his exasperation. "That old corral is strong enough to hold these critters overnight."

He swore again, disgustedly, and stomped away.

Jerry was still sitting his pony. He reined it into action to head back an obstreperous cow that had ideas about leaving the bunch and heading off on its own. Then he rode back to Wing.

Wing said to Jerry, "Well?"

Jerry laughed briefly. "Don't jump to any foolish conclusions, Shorty. I know what I'm doing."

Wing looked relieved. He hurried off and in a few minutes returned with Steve Hackett. Both were mounted now and they took over the job of getting the cows into the corral.

Jerry turned his pony into the saddlers' corral

and, after setting his saddle on one of the top bars, made his way to the cookhouse. Here he found Cornpone Jones bending over his range on which pots and pans bubbled and steamed. Jones was a bit unsteady on his feet, and there was a partly emptied bottle of whisky on the table.

Jones glanced up, scowled when he saw Jerry, "Get out of my kitchen," he ordered in his cracked voice.

"Just a minute, Cornpone," Jerry said mildly. "I just dropped in to see if I could do you a favor—"

"Heh! A favor! Bah! Like gettin' me to cook steaks, I suppose, if you butcher one of them beefs you drove in a spell back. Well, it's too late to make any changes in my menu now, I'd have you know—"

"You're all wrong, Cornpone. I was just going to see if I could tote some table fixin's to the bunkhouse for you. Cripes! That food smells tasty. I didn't have any dinner today."

"Whose fault is that? You should of took some bread and beans when you left. If you want to help, you can tote some dishes and knives and forks and so on. Then come back and get the coffeepot."

Jerry gathered the tableware and disappeared in the direction of the bunkhouse. In a minute he was back. "What's next?"

"You'll have to wait a mite. Coffee ain't boiled yet."

Jerry waited. Seeing a large pan of biscuits on the table, without asking leave, he reached over and took one, sunk his teeth into it, and then managed to tear a chunk loose.

"Lord in Heaven!" Jerry mumbled through a mouthful of soggy dough. "What a biscuit! I'll bet a high-toned hotel in Kansas City couldn't serve any better. Cornpone, you're a genius, when it comes to baking. Now if I only had some meat gravy to dunk 'em in—"

"Take another," Cornpone invited. "Mop it in this here pan. Glad you like 'em."

Jerry took another and "mopped" it in some bacon grease. Well, that did moisten it a bit. Privately, he decided if he ever went fishing, he'd get some of Cornpone's biscuits and use them as sinkers on the end of his line.

"Plumb elegant biscuits," Jerry prevaricated.

"I'd make you a pie, could I ever get Kelt to buy some dried apples or apricots," Jones cackled. "Take a drink of likker, if you like," he added generously.

"Thanks just the same," Jerry declined. "I don't like to drink before supper. Cornpone, on your wages, I don't see how you can afford so much liquor."

"Heh! heh!" the old cook laughed. "Don't cost me nothin'. Kelt buys it for me. I got him across the hip, and he knows it. He figures to keep me good-natured, or I might quit and spill a few things what I know."

"What sort of things?"

Cornpone hesitated, but the alcohol in his system prevented caution. "I seen you when you drove them cows in—Two-M cows, they was. And that ain't the first time that sort of crooked business has took place. Sometimes Jaklin brings 'em, or Beadle or Corwin. Once or twice, Kelt himself drove some in."

"Always Two-M cows?"

Cornpone shook his head. "Not always. Other brands too." He took a drink himself, holding the tilted bottle against his lips for quite a long drink. He shuddered and replaced the bottle on the table, wiped the back of his hand across his mouth. "It's just when it gets late in the day, they bring 'em here."

"Where do they take them?"

"Ain't—*hic!*—Kelt told you, yet? Well, he never told me, nuther, but ol' Cornpone keeps his ears open, he does. They herd them stole critters to Camino Canyon. What happens to them then, I dunno. I reckon Kelt sells 'em out of this territory. It's as I'm tellin' you, Kelt knows what I know, and he don't want me blabbin' to nobody. So he furnishes whisky to keep me satisfied here."

Cornpone started fishing boiled potatoes from

a pot and stacking them on a wide metal platter. "Here, you can put these spuds on the table. I'll have somethin' else to tote when you get back. But don't ever mention to Kelt what I've told you. He might cut off my likker supply."

"Or worse," Jerry told himself mentally.

At supper, Flecker directed questions to all the men there: had any of them heard Jacklin say where he intended going when he departed that morning. All shook their heads.

Corwin asked, "Didn't you give him orders, Kelt?" He looked at Flecker, then directed a swift glance toward Jerry, who was struggling with another biscuit, then back to Flecker again.

"Yeah, I did," Flecker said gruffly. "Don't know why he ain't back by this time. Maybe he misunderstood, or somethin'."

The men continued eating, but nobody had anything much to say. Cornpone entered, that is to say, he sort of staggered in, bearing a platter containing more food. At the table he set the platter down, then ranged his bleary vision along the table.

A frown came over Cornpone's features as he once more looked from man to man. Then started counting on his fingers.

"What in hell do you think you're doing, Cornpone?" Flecker demanded in some irritation.

Cornpone had started to count again on his

fingers. Now he paused. "There's one man missin'," he announced dramatically. "Where's—*hic!*—Herb Jacklin?"

"What are you, the mother-hen around here?" Flecker asked sarcastically. "Checkin' up on the crew? Go on, slope back to your kitchen."

"I like to know how many I—*hic!*—got to feed," Cornpone said defiantly. "Here I brung in more chow—you know yourownself he eats enough for two men—"

"That's his business," Flecker growled. "Now, get out!"

"But where is Jacklin? His hoss is out there, standin' nigh the corral—"

"What?" Flecker half-yelled, leaping up from the table. In his haste to get down to the saddlers' corral he almost trod the old cook underfoot and nearly skidded to a fall as he rounded the bunkhouse doorway.

The men ate in silence, awaiting Flecker's return. It was all clear to Jerry of course: the riderless horse had finally made its way home and was waiting to be unsaddled.

Five minutes later, Flecker returned, cursing. Corwin asked, "Jacklin not out there, Kelt?"

Scowling, Flecker shook his head. "Nowhere around. It's my guess his hoss threw him and he's walkin' back. Dammit to hell! I always warned him that hoss spooked easy and would take to buckin' if a loose piece of paper or a tumbleweed blew across his path. But Herb never would listen to reason. Swore the hoss didn't live that could sun his boot-soles. Well, mebbe now, he's learned his lesson."

Beadle nodded agreement. "Herb always was sort of stubborn that way. You couldn't tell him nothing—"

Flecker interrupted, "Knight, you were over that way today. You didn't see Jacklin walkin' across the range, did you?"

Jerry shook his head. "No," he responded truthfully. "I'd have mentioned it to you, if I had."

"In that case," Frank Reed put in, "I reckon Jerry would have picked him up and brought him in, or taken after the hoss—somethin' like that."

Beadle said thoughtfully, "Kelt, you don't suppose somebody might have shot Jacklin out of his saddle, do you?"

"And who would be liable to do that?" Flecker demanded.

Beadle shrugged. "One of them hoe-men might have drawed a bead on him and pulled trigger. They ain't got no love for the Circle-F."

Flecker shook his head. "I don't figure it that way. In the first place I don't think none of them farmers has enough money to own a gun, let alone knowin' how to shoot one straight. I admit somethin' like that occurred to me, for a minute. Then I looked over his saddle good, didn't see no blood or slug marks on it no place."

"Kelt," Jerry said gravely, "I told you I saw a couple of Two-M hands over that way. Do you reckon Jacklin run into some trouble with them. Leastwise, I took 'em for Two-M hands."

"I don't figure so"—Flecker brushed aside the question—"and there's no need, Knight, for you to mention where you was today—"

"What I was thinking," Jerry cut in, "maybe you could ride over to the Two-M and ask Monroe if he saw anything of Jacklin."

"Dammit!" Flecker growled. "That'd be just a waste of time. You leave all thinkin' to me, Knight. I'll decide what to do when the time comes. Naw"—hopefully—"Jacklin's hoss just throwed him, put him afoot. You'll see him come footin' it in by midnight, if not before, with his legs wore down to stumps. And won't I hoorah him about that hoss he said couldn't toss him." Flecker turned to Shorty Wing. "When you finish eatin', you go down and take care of Jacklin's bronc."

The meal continued in silence. The worried look didn't quite leave Flecker's features, though he blustered and cursed as usual when the meal was concluded.

# XI

The corraled Two-M cows were gathered right after breakfast the following morning, and Jerry saddled up and prepared for the drive to Camino Canyon. Tim Beadle and George Corwin also got into saddles, announcing they were going along with Jerry to show him the way to the canyon.

"Figuring I might get lost?" Jerry asked dryly.

Beadle said shortly, "No tellin'. Anyway, we got a job to do when we get there."

Jerry glanced back. He'd heard Flecker yelling at somebody. He saw Shorty Wing, Frank Reed and Steve Hackett saddling up. He spoke casually. "They figurin' to help me locate the way, too?"

Corwin supplied the answer. "Kelt got plumb worried about Herb Jacklin. Figured he might be layin' out on the range with a broke leg, or somethin' and couldn't make to walk home. He's sendin' them three waddies out to comb the range and see if they could find him somewhere."

"Could be he's layin' senseless," Beadle surmised. "A throwed hand could land on his head and—"

"C'mon," Corwin cut in, "let's get these cows out of that corral and on their way. We got a job to do."

The Two-M Herefords had already been

watered and caused no particular trouble while getting them lined out and started in a northeasterly direction. Within a short time, the Circle-F buildings were left to the rear beyond the first swell of land, and the animals grazed peacefully on the lush grass as they were herded slowly ahead. After a half hour or so, the cowboys urged them to a faster gait.

Still, the cows weren't hurried too much. "They still got a mite of trail to travel," Corwin offered. "No use runnin' any tallow off them."

The three men rode somewhat behind, so as not to be forced to swallow too much of the dust kicked up by the marching Herefords. Jerry rode in the middle, with Corwin and Beadle on either side of him. Now and then it became necessary for one of the riders to employ a swinging lariat as a lash to hustle on some lagging animal. All things considered, however, the cows caused little trouble and good time was being made.

"Lush grazing country," Jerry observed, hoping to start a conversation.

"None better," Beadle agreed. "And it continues even through the foothills of the San Lucias. Good country beyond the mountains, too."

Both Beadle and Corwin seemed a bit more friendly than they had been, Jerry mused. Now, what was the reason for that? Could it be they considered him like themselves, now that he had fallen in with Flecker's plans?

Various thoughts coursed through Jerry's mind as they pushed on. The sun was higher now and the riders began to perspire. To the west the sky was so blue it appeared almost black. The sun's rays cast long shadows before men and animals. Once the cows tried to halt in the shadow of some tall rocks and mesquite trees, but the riders forced them to keep going.

They were getting into gradually rising terrain by this time as the foothills now appeared nearer.

Corwin laughed suddenly. Jerry looked questioningly at him. Corwin explained, "Kelt was some uncertain about you, yesterday, Knight."

"How come?" Jerry queried.

"He had a feelin' you might cut your tail out of this country, once you were out of his sight."

"So what if I had?" Jerry asked.

"It's been the worse for you if you had," Beadle stated. "If you'd not showed up in due time, or we hadn't heard nothin' from you, word would have been sent to Deputy Drake, and he would have been told certain things about you."

"Aw," Jerry blustered, "Drake couldn't do nothing to me."

Corwin laughed sarcastically. "Kelt figures different, from what he told us—"

"He told you hombres about me?" Jerry bridled.

Corwin nodded. "He's got plenty on you, Knight."

"Why that son-of-a-pitch-me-over-a-corral-rail!" Jerry pretended to be angry.

"What d'you expect?" Beadle laughed. "Kelt don't miss much, and he keeps us posted."

"I suppose so." Jerry seemed to slump a little, then, "To be frank, I did consider lighting out, for a time."

"Why didn't you?" Corwin asked curiously.

"We-ell, I thought the matter over and thought what a damn fool I'd be, to leave a good job, with a chance of picking up extra money from time to time. And I could feel safe on the Circle-F, in a way."

The wind had shifted a trifle, and now the dust raised by the cows' trudging hooves was blown off to one side, making it more comfortable for the riders. One by one, they lowered the bandannas they'd tied across noses and mouths.

"To tell the truth," Beadle put in, "Kelt was plumb surprised to see you return—especially bringin' these cows. He never expected you. Threw quite a jolt into him when you showed up."

Corwin, in an effort to shut his partner up, growled, "Tim, I figure we should do less talkin' and get these cows delivered."

"We're makin' good time," Beadle said carelessly.

"But why," Jerry asked, "should Kelt be surprised at my return?"

Beadle suddenly changed the subject. "Like George says, we should prod these critters a mite. We're takin' too much time for a short drive like this."

"Or maybe," Jerry surmised, "I wasn't supposed to return."

Neither man replied. Corwin spurred his pony to action and, with swinging lariat, whipped across a cow's face, forced it back with the herd. He took his time returning to the others.

Beadle, in an endeavor to cover up the break he'd made, said, "Well, Knight, Kelt realized there was a chance you might run into some Two-M riders and have trouble."

Jerry said indignantly, "Well, that's a hell of a way to treat a new hand. He might've warned me."

Beadle shook his head. "That ain't Kelt's way. He wanted to test you out, see how tough you are, case you ran into trouble. If you ride with the Circle-F, you got to show guts. Otherwise, Kelt won't have you. But you stick with us, cowboy, and you'll pick up plenty extra money, 'fore you're through."

Corwin rejoined the two and Beadle fell silent. Corwin asked casually, "Knight, when you got these cows, yesterday, didn't you run into any trouble at all? Nobody took a shot at you or nothin'?"

"Did you think I would?" Jerry asked.

Corwin shrugged. "There's always that chance."

"I reckon," Jerry acknowledged. "But, like I told Kelt, there was a couple of riders over that way, so I hid out behind some rocks until they'd left."

Corwin didn't pursue the subject further.

The cows were rounding a low hill, now. Here there seemed to be a well-worn trail. Gradually they climbed, up one hill and then down another. By this time the San Lucia Mountains seemed to tower almost overhead, peaks etched ruggedly against the blue sky. There were more big outcroppings of rock on either side. The rocks closed in as animals and riders advanced, then suddenly opened up.

"Camino Canyon," Beadle announced. "Now you'll be able to find it alone next time, Knight."

The three riders closed in on the cows, urging them into the deep canyon, whose sloping walls were covered with grass, brush and scrub oak. Rounding a bend in the canyon, Jerry saw some hundred and fifty or more Two-M cows, penned up in a crude corral, built of limbs, loose rock and cottonwood trunks. One end of the corral dipped to a small waterhole.

This trail through the canyon appeared little frequented and the corral was partly screened by tall brush and cottonwood trees, so there was little likelihood of the rustled beefs being discovered by anyone unless he were led to the spot.

There were a couple of ponies tethered near the corral and as the cows were driven in, two men rose, on foot, and advanced to meet them. Both were hard-bitten individuals with unshaven jaws and belligerent appearances. Scarred forty-five six-shooters were suspended from their cartridge belts. They wore the usual range attire, sombreros, denim pants, boots, woollen shirts.

"These Circle-F hands too?" Jerry asked, as the two men approached.

Beadle shook his head. "They sort of work with us, you might say, though. Once across a county line, they'll take charge of the cows. They'll deal with Kelt later."

"Sure holding a bunch of Two-M critters here." Jerry pretended to be surprised. "You fellers must have been right busy on Two-M range lately."

"Naw." Beadle laughed. He gave Jerry a wink. "These is just a few strays that have wandered over this way from time to time. We've been holdin' 'em here for quite a spell. In case any Two-M hand did discover this spot, we could always say their critters strayed over this way and we was just holdin' 'em, until they could be returned proper, when we had time." He winked again.

Jerry laughed. "Your explanation is clear as mud, unless you could get the Two-M to believe it."

"I don't figure the Two-M is goin' to have a

chance to question it. These cows are due to be moved out right now. George and me will go along with these two hombres comin', and help drive 'em over the line. Then we'll be comin' back to the Circle-F. You can head back to the ranch right now, Knight. You ain't needed no more."

The horses had been drawn to a stop. The two men who'd been waiting in the canyon now drew abreast, looking questioningly at Jerry.

"This is Jinglebob and Pistol-foot," Corwin announced. "Brothers. Never heard their last names." He jerked one hand toward Jerry. "Name's Knight. He's okay. Just doesn't want to meet any lawmen, that's all."

The two men nodded in surly fashion to Jerry. He gave them a scowl in reply.

Jinglebob turned to Corwin. "The corral's going to be right full—" he growled.

"No it won't," Corwin stated. "We're clearin' all the cows out right now. Kelt wants the canyon clean should anybody get snoopy and ride this way."

"Hell!" Pistol-foot growled. "You can't clear out all the sign."

Corwin laughed slyly. "Sign doesn't have any brands on it. So let's get going. Tim and I will come along to help you."

"This is goddamn short notice—" Pistol-foot began.

His brother cut him short. "It's a good idea, I figure. We been runnin' shy on supplies anyway."

Corwin turned back to Jerry. "You head back and tell Kelt we got here okay, and Tim and I'll be back just as soon as we get a receipt for this stuff."

Jerry nodded and turned his pony. A few minutes later he had left the others far behind as he loped around the bend in the canyon, the pony's hooves striking sparks from bits of loose rock every now and then, the sounds echoing from the canyon walls as he traveled.

# XII

Kelt Flecker caught the sounds of the pony's hoof-thuds when Jerry rode in that afternoon, around three o'clock. He came striding down to the corral while Jerry was unsaddling the chestnut pony.

Without preliminaries he said, "Get there all right?"

Jerry nodded. Before he could continue, Flecker asked, "Meet any other riders on the trail?"

Jerry shook his head. "Not none. Saw a couple of hands, new to me, in the canyon. Pistol-foot and Jinglebob—"

"Yeah, a couple of no-good crooks, but they fit in my plans, and take care of things the other side of the line. Mean bastards! The kind of hombres that'll plug a man just to see which way he'll fall, after they've laid bets on the direction the corpse will take."

"Figured 'em that way," Jerry replied. "And Corwin and Beadle are going along to help 'em herd the cows over the line. Said to tell you they'd be back as soon as they got a receipt for the herd."

"Them was my orders. They like as not won't get home till tomorrow night—quite a drive ahead of 'em."

Jerry asked, "Did Herb Jacklin get back?"

"No, dammit, he didn't," Flecker growled. "He must have got hurt bad, when his hoss throwed him."

"No word from Wing, Hackett or Reed, eh?"

Flecker shook his head. Again that anxious look crept into his features. "Howsomever, if they're scannin' the range good, you can't expect to hear from 'em this soon, not less one of 'em found Herb right off. Could be they'd have to make a litter to carry him on, too. That'd take time."

"I suppose it would," Jerry said thoughtfully.

Flecker swung abruptly away, then hesitated. "When you get finished with that bronc, come down to the bunkhouse."

Jerry rubbed down the chestnut with his saddle-blanket and then watered the animal. Turning it into the saddlers' corral, he hoisted his saddle to a top bar of the corral and then wended his way to the bunkhouse.

Flecker was seated at his desk when Jerry entered. The big man stooped beneath his desk and came up with a bottle of whisky. "Like as not," he growled, "you'll want a snack from Cornpone, after missin' your dinner. He'll try to take your head off until he sees this bottle."

"The bottle for Cornpone?"

"Yeah. If I don't keep his skin soaked, he might quit on me. We need him here." Flecker gave a sly grin. "I watered this down some, but he'll never know the difference. And tell him not to bring no supper in, until the other boys—and Herb Jacklin—get home."

Jerry made his way to the cookhouse. Cornpone was seated at the table, head on arms, sound asleep. A few peeled potatoes and a bucket of water stood near. His customary whisky bottle stood empty on the table. A bucket of unpeeled potatoes was set next to it.

Jerry kept his hands behind his back and spoke. "Hey, cookie!"

Cornpone didn't stir, beyond emitting a long-drawn snore.

Jerry repeated the call. Cornpone tried to shake his head. "Go 'way," he muttered. Finally he opened bleary eyes and tried to focus them on Jerry. "Go 'way," he mumbled, "can't be bothered when I'm stirrin' 'lasses cake . . ." The words ran off in an indistinct mutter that said something about bacon grease and flour.

"Come awake, Cornpone!" Jerry said sharply.

Now the cook's rolling eyes came to a stop and he made out Jerry's form. "Oh, it's you," he scowled.

"Cornpone, I didn't have any dinner."

"That's your own tough luck. Now get out, I got my spuds to peel."

"How's for a sandwich, cookie?"

"You can wait till supper."

"How's for a sandwich, cookie?" Jerry repeated, drawing the bottle from behind his back.

That was the charm that worked. "That for me, Knight?"

"In return for one sandwich. That's my price. What have you got?"

Cornpone was wide awake now, eyes eagerly following the bottle.

"We-ell, I just ain't certain," he said. "Might be if I had a drink I could think a mite better."

Jerry removed the cork and held out the bottle. Cornpone reached for it, but Jerry kept a firm hold while he held the bottle to the cook's lips a moment. Then he jerked it away. Whisky dribbled down the oldster's chin, but his eyes were brighter now.

"That help your thinking?" Jerry grinned.

"It was mighty satisfactual." Cornpone nodded. "Now, lemme see. I got some cold beans. Mashed on chunks of sourdough, with catsup on 'em, makes a prime sandwich. An' could be I can open a can of sardines and 'nother of peaches." He struggled up from the chair, saying, "I'll build up the fire and get some coffee boilin'. That should hold you till suppertime."

"Fine. Oh, yes. Kelt says he don't want no supper put on until the other boys get in, with Herb Jacklin, but God knows when that will be."

Cornpone uttered an oath. "Sometimes Kelt don't show no more sense than a little kid playing with a string o' spools. I don't mind holdin' up the chow a mite, but I don't figger to wait all night. Hell's-bells on a tomcat! Don't Kelt realize I gotta lot of readyin' up after supper—dishes to wash an' so on?"

"I'm merely relayin' Kelt's orders," Jerry said mildly.

"Geez! I'm not criticizin' you," Cornpone stated wrathfully. "It's thet Kelt Flecker. He acts like he was a god or somethin'." He seized the bottle and took a sizable swig from the contents.

"How about that sandwich?" Jerry hinted.

"I ain't forgot." Cornpone went to the range and shoved in a couple of sticks of kindling, then blew on the embers to start a blaze. He poured water into a coffeepot, then proceeded to mash cold beans on a thick chunk of sourdough bread, which he then doused with catsup. Next he opened a can of sardines and another of canned peaches which he placed before Jerry.

"Set you down and eat hearty," he invited genially. "Here's a chunk of rat-trap cheese you may want, too. That coffee'll be ready in a few minutes."

From time to time the old cook had recourse to the bottle of whisky while Jerry settled to the food placed before him.

"You sure can put out a tasty snack when you set your mind to it," Jerry complimented, through a mouthful of food. "I'm plumb surprised you aren't working for some top-notch outfit."

"You're speakin' God's own truth," Cornpone replied. "Trouble is, Kelt don't appreciate good cookin'. Someday I'm goin' to quit the outfit cold." He poured steaming coffee into a tin mug and shoved a can of condensed milk in Jerry's direction. "You know"—seriously—"I've seen so much dirty work round here, that sometimes I get to frettin'. I figure that someday the law might shut down on Kelt Flecker, and hit him right where it hurts. He acts like he's God A'mighty, though."

"That so?" Jerry asked. "Suppose the law did catch up with Kelt. What would you do? You don't know much of anything."

"T'hell you say," Cornpone bristled. "I got eyes, ain't I? An' ears to listen with. I knows what's goin' on, with other owner's beef bein' drove up to Camino Canyon. What happens after that, I ain't sure, but I've noticed some strange rider a month or so later—I think I heard him called Jinglebob—ride in and give Kelt money. Even seen him countin' it one night, after this Jinglebob hombre came here. It's my guess then Kelt splits that money with that Capron hombre manager, but I can't say for certain." He paused, scowling. "I'd like to bet a plugged *peso* that it ain't an even split, nuther. An' I notice that Jacklin and Corwin an' Beadle has extra cash too, after that Jinglebob feller has been here. But me"—disgruntledly—"I never see none o' that extra cash. I'm just expected to get along on my same ol' fifty a month. Kelt can sure be tight with money, sometimes."

Jerry took a bite of his sandwich, washed it down with a sardine and a swig of hot coffee. "Supposing," he asked idly, "the law did close down on Flecker sometime and it come to a court case and they questioned you. What would you do?"

"Me?" Cornpone took another drink from the whisky bottle. "Natural, I wouldn't know nothing. I'm just a cook." He gave Jerry a bleary wink. "Me, I'm loyal to the outfit that pays me wages. Just so long's I keep my own skin clear, I don't care what happens."

"Yeah, I know," Jerry pursued. "I can understand that. But if it came to a matter of saving your skin or Kelt Flecker's skin, would you still claim you knew nothing?"

"T'hell I would!" Cornpone exclaimed. "Kelt ain't nothin' to me. I'd talk plenty to save my own skin."

"I figure you're smart." Jerry nodded. He dropped the subject, saying, "Here, I'll finish peeling these spuds for you."

"Damned if you ain't a help in a man's kitchen," Cornpone said gratefully. He staggered a little. "My rheumaticks is sort a raisin' hell o'late, sort a slows me up a mite. Them beans soakin' in the pot over there"—he dropped heavily into a chair—"I'd be obliged if you'd salt 'em and put the pot on the stove. You might stick a few more sticks of wood in the range. When that's done, there's a pan of Brown George"—meaning a doughy mess of flour, ginger and molasses—"you can stick in the oven to bake. When that's done, I'd be obliged if you'd cut some slices from that sowbelly hangin' overhead. Later you can set it to fryin' in the big skillet, hangin' from the wall there. An' there's them beans to warm up . . ."

Cornpone reached for the bottle, leaving it to Jerry to prepare the supper. In a few minutes, head on his arms on the table, he was fast asleep. Jerry smiled commiserately on the old cook and opened another can of peaches, to add to those left in the can from which he'd been eating. Then with flour and bacon grease he rolled out some dough and arranged it in two pie-tins he'd found, with the proper amount of sugar, ending up by placing in the oven two peach pies.

He washed up a few dishes and then, leaving Cornpone to his nap, left the cookhouse, secure now in the feeling that if a showdown came, Cornpone would be ready to testify to certain skulduggeries taking place on the Circle-F Ranch and environs.

He sauntered down to the saddlers' corral and looked over his black gelding. The pony appeared fit to travel again, after its rest, and greeted Jerry with an eager nicker.

"You're looking fit, hoss," Jerry said. "If I ride tomorrow, it's you I'll be saddling."

It was after dark when Reed, Shorty Wing and Steve Hackett arrived, one by one. None of them had seen any evidence of Herb Jacklin's body, alive or otherwise, in their search.

"You must have missed him," Flecker stated doggedly. "Like as not he was behind one of them rocks over that way, waitin' for some help to get him back."

"Could be," Frank Reed conceded. "I've talked to Shorty and Steve and we sure scoured the range. We fanned out in different directions, and looked careful. All's we saw was our Circle-F cows over that way. We didn't look on Two-M holdin's, of course."

"Not likely he'd be found on Two-M," Flecker said quickly. "I've give all our hands orders to keep off Two-M property—we don't want to have trouble with Monroe. He might think if any of his hands saw my men there, we was up to no good. Got to keep on friendly relations with the Two-M, as you hombres know."

They nodded, they knew.

Flecker's scowl deepened. Stubbornly, he said, "I just know that Jacklin is layin' out there someplace—like as not too injured to call out, should any rider happen to pass."

"I figure," Jerry put in, "Jacklin might have had some trouble."

"What sort of trouble?" Flecker demanded, glowering.

"Well," Jerry explained his statement, "after you sent Shorty to take care of Jacklin's bronc, I examined his rifle in the saddle-boot. I found three cartridges had been fired, anyway—'course I don't know if he had a full magazine when he left here. Could be even more shots had been fired—"

"Goddammit!" Flecker said wrathfully. "Why'n't you say so before?"

"You never asked," Jerry said mildly. "I didn't aim to cross you when you felt so sure his horse had thrown him. You know yourownself, Kelt, you said you made all the decisions round here. Maybe the horse bucked him off, like you said—"

"I never claimed that hoss was a bucker," Flecker said wrathfully. "I just said it spooked easy, was skittish. I don't think that bronc could be made to buck. I 'member the day Herb took all the buckin' outta him. The hoss bucked Herb off—just once. Then Herb got back in the saddle and took to beatin' it over the head with a loaded quirt every time it moved sudden. Nope, that hoss was sure broke of buckin'. Nope, I'm certain in my mind that the hoss made a sudden start, takin' Herb unawares and throwed him." Doggedly, he adhered to his opinion. "Herb's sure as hell layin' out there, waitin' for some help to come. I'm beginnin' to think now that he's hurt real bad."

"That must be it," Jerry conceded gravely.

What more might have been said was interrupted by the entrance of Cornpone Jones, entering the bunkhouse with dishes and tableware.

"I could appreciate it," Cornpone grumbled, "if a couple you lazy cow-nurses would gimme a hand totin' in the chow."

Shorty Wing and Jerry arose to give the old cook a hand. Within a short time the steaming food was placed on the table and the men commenced to eat. Only Flecker seemed to have lost his appetite. It was plain to see he was worried about Herb Jacklin's disappearance, though he didn't reopen the subject. The men ate in silence, all but Jerry forming surmises in their minds as to Jacklin's failure to appear, and none of them arriving at a correct solution.

Within a short time, Cornpone staggered in again. "Got a treat for y'all tonight," he stated brazenly, with no word of credit for Jerry's work. "I baked you a coupla *de-lic-ious* peach pies." He glanced guiltily a moment at Jerry. "What do you think o' that, Kelt?"

"Anything you cook stinks," Flecker growled. "Go get me some more coffee, and don't talk so much."

"One more incidence of love's labor lost," Cornpone said defiantly, and managed to make the turn at the open doorway without bumping into anything.

Supper was finally concluded. The men rose from the table. Flecker sat as before, biting his lower lip, a scowl creasing his forehead.

Abruptly, Flecker said, "Just a minute, you hombres." They waited. Then to Jerry he continued, "I got a job for you, tomorrow, Knight."

"Yeah?" Jerry queried. "Like I did yesterday?"

Flecker shook his head. "You did elegant, yesterday," he stated grudgingly. "I ain't kickin'. But this is different. I want you to take Reed, Wing and Hackett and head over that way and really scour the country for Herb Jacklin. I feel sure he's there, if you'll look well. I want you all to search behind every rock in sight. You'll be in charge, Knight. You know that country now—"

Jerry said, "What makes you so sure Jacklin's over that way, Kelt? Did you send him in that direction?"

Flecker hesitated. "Well, he was headed that way when he left here. I want him found," he said finally.

"We'll do the best we can," Jerry said. "Should we scour Two-M holdin's too?"

Flecker hesitated. "If there ain't no Two-M riders in sight. It's up to you." He repeated, "I want Jacklin found. Hell, if he's disappeared there's no tellin'—" He broke off abruptly. "You got my orders. That's all."

The men filed out of the bunkhouse and didn't stop until they'd halted near the saddlers' corral. They looked questioningly at Jerry.

Shorty Wing laughed. "Knight, it looks like you've risen in Flecker's favor."

"What gives you that idea."

"He said plain you were to be in charge, when we ride to look for Jacklin tomorrow."

"You objecting?" Jerry smiled.

Frank Reed put in, "None of us are objecting, Jerry. It's just that we're surprised at Flecker turning the deal over to you, like he figured you were to be trusted with his ideas."

"Maybe that's Flecker's idea," Jerry said. "That doesn't mean I'm all sold out to him."

Steve Hackett said, "We scoured the range good today. You got any idea where Herb Jacklin is to be found?"

"At present, not the slightest," Jerry said. "I know where he was yesterday, but since then—well, I don't know what's happened."

"You're saying too much or too little," Reed stated bluntly. "Just where are we expected to look for—?"

"Forget Jacklin," Jerry said shortly. "We'll leave to look for Jacklin, as Flecker orders, but we're not going to find him."

"You talk right sure," Hackett said, looking puzzled.

"I know what I'm talking about," Jerry assured him.

Wing said, "Jerry, what's your game? If we don't look for Jacklin, what are we ridin' for?"

"To square a debt," Jerry said promptly. "The Circle-F has stolen some two hundred Two-M cows. There's a nice bunch of Circle-F beefs over that way. We four are going to cut out two hundred head of Circle-F animals and deliver 'em to Monroe's outfit. In that way, we keep the account balanced."

His statement was met with wide stares and dropped jaws.

"That is," Jerry added, "if you three hombres are game to side me in the deal."

"What?" The three voices came as one, in unbelievable tones.

"You heard me, waddies. Are you with me or not?"

The three looked at one another. They had started to nod, rather dumbly, but unquestioningly, when Reed asked, "Jerry, what in hell kind of game are you playing?"

"A damned dangerous one, perhaps. I warn you, this may result in some gun-throwing before we get through. If you want to steer clear of the deal, I won't hold it against you. But I'm laying it on the line, so you'll know what we're bucking.

So it's up to you to decide. Are you with me or against me? Just keep it in your mind that I'm out to stop Flecker and his crooked deals."

The other three glanced quickly at each other. A silent, affirmative vote seemed to be taken. Frank Reed nodded. "Anything to stop Flecker is okay with us, Jerry. We're with you, of course. But we're still itchin' to know exactly what all this is about."

Jerry nodded. "Flecker is worried plenty because Jacklin hasn't showed up. He's on pins and needles trying to figure things out. I've got a hunch he's afraid that Jacklin might have double-crossed him some way, and he's worryin' a heap."

Steve Hackett asked, "You any idea what happened to Jacklin?"

Jerry nodded soberly, then threw his bomb. "I killed the scut."

The statement was met with surprised gasps and explosive exclamations. The three gazed wide-eyed at the information.

Jerry explained. "Flecker sent me rustling Two-M cows in hope I'd get shot while I was doing it. He sent Jacklin to spy on me, learn what happened. I met a girl over there, from the Two-M—"

"Alice Monroe, I suppose," Shorty Wing guessed.

Jerry nodded. "Miss Alice Monroe. She was plenty suspicious of me at first and—well, to make a long story short, we got acquainted and I learned a few things from her, so she has some inkling of what I'm trying to do. As I figure it, Jacklin was spying on me from a nearby hillside, and he saw the girl and I were talking friendly sort of. That didn't suit Jacklin. Maybe he suspected I wasn't following out orders as Flecker had given them. So, he threw down on me with his rifle. I was lucky he didn't hit me. It was damn close. I rode up the hillside after him, located him in a thicket of brush and we shot it out with six-shooters. I was lucky. Then I slapped his horse on the rump, knowing it would come back here eventually. I aimed to upset Flecker and I reckon I have."

"I'll be everlastingly damned!" Hackett exclaimed.

"Maybe we all will be," Jerry said dryly, "or get filled with lead slugs, which amounts to the same thing, in a way. We've still got Flecker, Corwin and Beadle to handle—all mean men with a hawg-laig. And there's a pair of murderous scuts of brothers over at Camino Canyon—Jinglebob and Pistol-foot, they're called—"

"They was here once," Shorty Wing remembered, "couple months or more back. Sure, they'd throw in with Flecker, I'm bettin'. Poisonous rattlers, both of 'em. Pistol-foot knocked Cornpone Jones down because he didn't like the coffee, he said. Cornpone went back to his kitchen and then returned with a shotgun loaded with buckshot. Kelt smoothed the trouble over by givin' Cornpone a bottle of likker."

Jerry nodded. "Pistol-foot struck me as being just that kind of a bustard. Tomorrow, when we ride over that way, I'm expecting to meet Alice Monroe and her father. Could be they'll have other hands with 'em. Anyway, one way or another, I figure there'll be lead thrown plumb promiscuous when the showdown comes, and Flecker sees we're bucking him."

"And just about that time," Reed said seriously, "it looks like this range will be fogged plenty with powder smoke."

Steve Hackett commented shrewdly, "There's somethin' here that don't quite dovetail in my mind."

"What's that?" Jerry asked.

Steve explained. "I've seen enough of Jacklin to learn that he never does much on his own, without orders from Flecker. Now, it just ain't like Jacklin to throw a rifle shot at you, when he saw you talkin' to Alice Monroe. It'd be more his way to come back and tell Flecker what he saw, before he acted on his own thataway."

"Possible." Jerry nodded. "Flecker had two bets down—if I came back with the stolen cows, he was that much ahead. If he'd given Jacklin orders to plug me, he'd win there, too. Flecker figured he couldn't lose, no matter what happened."

“But, why”—Shorty Wing frowned—“should Flecker want you gunned down—so long as you could prove handy at stealin’ Two-M cattle?”

“I think,” Jerry replied slowly, “I’ve got that figured out, too. When things are clearer in my own mind, I’ll explain. Until then, let’s drop the subject. We’ll see how things turn out tomorrow—when we go looking for Jacklin.”

# XIII

It was close to noontime, the following day, when Jerry, on his black gelding, accompanied by the mounted Wing, Hackett and Reed, pushed some two hundred head of sleek Circle-F cattle across Aliso Creek and onto Two-M range. There was a short wait while the cows stopped to drink, the men heading the first arrivals somewhat downstream so they wouldn't muddy the water for the animals that came later.

They weren't pushing the cows too hard, and while they waited for the cattle to finish drinking, they took the opportunity to devour sandwiches they'd brought with them and roll and light Durham cigarettes.

Once the beefs had drunk their fill and begun to scatter, the men settled to their saddles again and got the beasts lined out, heading them in a more northwesterly direction. The herd moved along docilely enough, with the riders keeping them on the go and only now and then being forced to drive would-be wanderers back on the line of march.

It was going on to three o'clock when the herd approached the point on Two-M holdings where Jerry had talked to Alice Monroe, the day before yesterday. Looking ahead, Jerry saw four horses and, standing near them, four riders. One of them he guessed to be Alice.

Jerry called to Steve Hackett and the others, "Keep this herd going, boys. You'll catch up in a short time."

Then he spurred ahead. It was Alice, he saw as he drew nearer, though today the girl wore a green corduroy divided skirt. The man next to her, he judged to be her father—a tall spare man with grizzled hair and a short beard, dressed in cowman togs, holstered gun at side. The other two men he judged to be Two-M hands. They too wore the usual cowman clothing.

Jerry chuckled. "Looks like Monroe didn't know exactly what to expect, so he brought some reinforcements, case there was trouble of some kind."

The four had again mounted when Jerry drew abreast. "Hi-yuh, Alice," he greeted cheerfully. "I'll bet this is your dad."

"Afternoon, Jerry"—the girl smiled—"and you bet on a sure thing. Dad, this is Jerry Knight. Jerry, I've already told him you're crazy. Perhaps now he'll believe it, if he'll listen to you talk a spell."

Jerry reined the black gelding nearer and stuck out his hand. Mart Monroe accepted it somewhat dubiously, but had to admit, inwardly, he liked the firm grasp Jerry gave him, liked the direct way Jerry's gaze met his own.

Monroe bent piercing blue eyes on Jerry. "Young man," he said curtly, "I'm not goin' to say I'm pleased to meet you, until I know more about you." He gestured toward the Two-M hands, sitting their horses nearby. "Two of my men, Reece Yeagle and Todd Orcutt."

Jerry saluted them with a wave of one hand, and they nodded shortly in reply. He could see they were holding judgment in abeyance until more was learned about this strange cowboy. Both were lean, bronzed sons of the range, mature men who had their employer's best interests at heart.

"Look here, Knight," Monroe asked, eyes on the approaching line of marching Circle-F cows, kicking up a line of dust that almost threw Hackett, Reed and Wing into obscurity, "may I ask exactly what is the meaning behind those cattle I see being driven on Two-M range?"

"They're Circle-F critters," Jerry explained easily. "We figured to throw 'em over here—"

"Well, damn, I believe you are touched in the head," Monroe exploded wrathfully. "If you think you can bring your steers to graze on Two-M range, you're just as crazy as Alice said you were. The Circle-F has plenty good grass. Look here, did Flecker order you to bring them animals over on our land—?"

"Nope." Jerry grinned. "He don't even know it. It was just a sort of an idea I got myownself."

"I—I don't understand." Monroe scowled. "Maybe you figure 'cause you could pull the wool over Alice's eyes, you could fool me too. I want an explanation, right now, or you can tell those hands to turn them cows back where they come from. And I don't want any shenanigans from you—"

"Dad!" Alice interposed. "Give Jerry a chance to explain."

Scowling, Monroe snapped, "All right, Knight, start explainin' and be damn fast about it."

"First, you can call it a fair exchange," Jerry said quietly. "Mr. Monroe, did you know about two hundred of your cows were driven over the county line, yesterday, by Circle-F hands?"

Monroe's eyes bugged out. "What's that you're sayin'?" he half yelled.

"I'm telling you. Your cows have been picked off a few head at a time by the Circle-F, and held in Camino Canyon. Yesterday they were started, and will probably be sold with phony bills of sale."

A lot of the wind seemed taken out of Monroe's sails at such news. His manner changed to one of anger toward the Circle-F. "If what you say is God's truth, I'm going to ride in and see Deputy Drake—"

"I'm asking that you let that go for a spell," Jerry requested earnestly, "until we can get this whole business settled. Meanwhile, here's two hundred animals to take the place of those stolen from you. I'm asking that you throw 'em someplace where they won't be found at once—say, some miles farther on. You see, I hated to see you lose any critters. This is the quickest way I know to make your loss good."

"But—but—but I can't do this," Monroe gasped. "I can't accept these cows. It wouldn't be legal."

"We're making it legal." Jerry smiled. He drew from his pocket a sheet of paper with written words on it. "Here's a bill of sale for two hundred head."

Scowling, Monroe took the paper, read the words on it. He appeared about ready to explode. His face, above the beard, was scarlet. "By God," he roared, "Alice was right. You are batty in the head. Your name is signed to this paper. You haven't any right to sell Circle-F cows—"

"But don't you see," Jerry asked earnestly, "that paper clears you if any trouble should arise. If trouble does come, it descends on my head. All I ask is that you take these cows over to your holdings, and keep 'em, until this business is cleared up."

Somewhat reluctantly, Monroe folded the paper and placed it in his pocket. Then he had a new thought. "Say, are you a range detective from the Association—?"

"No," Jerry said promptly. "Though there

are times I wish I was. Will you do as I say?"

"Damned if I like it," Monroe grunted, "but I'll play along with you until I learn what your game is, but so help me, Knight, if you're not throwing a straight rope, I aim—personal—to let daylight through you—"

"Dad!" Alice broke in.

"You let be, Alice," he grunted. "I know what I'm doing—or maybe"—a ghost of a smile broke through his grizzled whiskers—"could be neither Knight or I know what we're doing. But I'll hold those cows until something breaks."

"Fine," Jerry said, "so we'll keep the herd moving then. If you'll tell your hands to lend a rope, my pards will go along to help until they get the cows through those hills."

Monroe gave orders to his men, who looked rather surprised, but spurred ponies to meet the cows. Monroe's riders stopped near Hackett a moment, then the drive continued on past Alice, her father and Jerry.

Jerry yelled after the Circle-F hands, "I'll stick around here until you come back."

They watched the herd slowly wending its way through the hills a few minutes, then Jerry turned to Monroe. "Could be that Flecker will send me to steal some more of your cows in a few days. I'd appreciate it if you'd warn your men not to throw down on me. I promise, any cows stolen from you, will be replaced."

"With more of the same sort of faked bills of sale, I suppose," Monroe grunted. He still appeared uneasy about the transaction. "I don't know as I like such doin's. It might make trouble."

"Sure." Jerry nodded. "I'm expecting that—trouble for Kelt Flecker. The things I've heard about that hombre sure rile my blood, and I'm out to break up his dirty game. He's taken advantage of a lot of poor farmers, I understand—him and Bristol Capron."

"But why," Monroe was insisting, "can't we just tell Deputy Drake what's been goin' on? That would settle Flecker's hash."

"Sure, but will it return property those poor hoe-men are about to lose? I want to get more proof against Flecker before I move."

Alice eyed him. "What are you, Jerry, some sort of crusader, riding around and trying to correct the ills of the world?"

Jerry laughed. "That's a mite too much territory for me to take in. If I can just correct the wrongs done in the name of the Randall Company, I'll feel I've made a start, anyway."

"You're sure carving out a big job for yourself, Jerry. And you're running big risks."

Jerry shrugged his wide shoulders. "What have I got to lose? I just like to stop crooks, that's all. Put it that way. Mr. Monroe, do you reckon it would be possible to get the names of the folks that have lost money through the Randall Company? You should be right well acquainted in Topango Wells."

Dubiously, Monroe shook his head. "You could get the names of folks who are still in this part of the country, I suppose, but a good many families, broke and discouraged, have moved out. There might be a chance at the county seat, if Bristol ever recorded property transactions—which same I doubt."

"I'll appreciate it if you can pick up any names. What you can't get, I may have to get from Bristol Capron."

Monroe laughed scornfully. "Capron wouldn't tell you anything."

Jerry said, a bit grimly, "There's more ways than one of skinning a coyote."

"Now don't you go makin' fool talk. Capron's more powerful than you. He could frame you into a killin'. You don't dast go too far."

"That's my risk," Jerry stated determinedly. "I just feel sort of sorry for those poor farmers."

Monroe nodded. "You and me both. I'd like to see 'em make a go of it. It would be right pleasurable to be able to buy some greens and garden truck from time to time. But they ain't got a chance, without water. Now, if Aliso Creek was dammed up—you know, I even suggested that to Flecker one time. I was even willin' to build up a dam on my property, but the creek is the dividin' line between the Two-M and Circle-F, and Flecker wouldn't even listen to my proposition. Claimed all the water was needed for his cows."

"We're thinking alike, anyhow," Jerry said. "I had something the same thing in mind." He changed the subject. "You didn't happen to find a dead skunk on that hill up there, did you?"

"We certain did," Monroe said emphatically. "Jerry, you sure placed your slugs close together—or somebody did. I forgot. Alice said I wasn't to mention your name. Well, I'll hold my lips just as long's possible, but I'll have to tell the truth, if I was to be put under oath, you understand. Not that I have any sympathy for a skunk like Jacklin. He was reckoned to be fast with a gun too, but looks like somebody was faster."

"Fast enough," Jerry nodded noncommittally. "What did you do?"

"Soon's Alice got home and told me 'bout you and what had happened—and I thought for a spell she'd gone as crazy as she said you appeared—I took a coupla my hands and we rode out to look for the body. It was gettin' dark, so we'd brung lanterns—needed 'em too before we got through. Quite a task searchin' through all that brush."

"I reckon it was." Jerry nodded. He waited for Monroe to go on.

"Well, as you know, there's a law against movin' a dead body. There wasn't much we could do. We threw some blankets over Jacklin's corpse, piled rocks on it, so's the coyotes wouldn't disturb nothin'. Just to make extra safe, I left one of the hands to guard the body overnight. Then, first thing yesterday mornin', I sent a cowhand ridin' to Topango Wells to tell Buck Drake. Then I rode back where I'd left my hand on guard, told him to go on back to the ranch and catch up on his shut-eye. Then I stayed."

"Deputy Drake come right out, I suppose."

"Buck got here quick, too. Good man, Buck Drake. He knows his duty. Buck took one look at the body, identified it as Herb Jacklin's, muttered something about him bein' no great loss to the community, then covered the body with the blanket again. Then he started grillin' me. Seein' Jacklin was found dead on Two-M range, I think he suspected that I or one of my men had killed Jacklin. I think he still half suspects somebody from the Two-M was responsible." Monroe drew a long sigh. "So I told a lie for you, Jerry."

"I plumb regret ruining your morals," Jerry said dryly.

Monroe gave a wry smile. "I reckon most of my morals was already ruined by the time I was your age."

"Dad!" Alice exclaimed. "That's no thing to say—"

Monroe laughed. "Let be, daughter. Jerry knows I was just joshin'. Not wantin' to implicate any of my boys, I told Buck that I was huntin' a stray over this way when I run across Jacklin's body. He gave me a sort of funny look, like he didn't believe me, but he didn't argue with me none about it."

"You know," Jerry pointed out, "you don't need to stick to that lie, Mr. Monroe."

"And I ain't aimin' to, should I be put under oath, nuther." Monroe stated. "But I'll ride along with your idea, until some sort of showdown comes."

"Thanks."

"*Por nada*—for nothing. Just tryin' to help." Monroe paused to gather his thoughts. "Then Buck began searchin' for sign in the vicinity of the body, lookin' for empty gun shells. Didn't find none, though, which seemed to surprise him. I expect if he could have found an empty he'd have tried to match it with a spent shell from my gun, or one of my men's. He started to cast about in wider circles, while I waited to see what he'd locate. Finally he came back with a coupla hoss hairs from what he thought was a chestnut—say, what kind of a horse are you ridin'?"

"My black gelding," Jerry said. "Today. Two days ago I was forking a chestnut from our saddlers' corral."

"Might be a good idea to check the chestnut's left rear hoof. A bad worn shoe at that point. Maybe you'd best change it."

"Thanks, but I'll let it ride for a spell."

"That's up to you. Buck Drake also found where another hoss had waited, but he couldn't get much sign—nothin' but dry brush and leaves there. A few broken branches but that didn't tell him anything. He examined Jacklin's six-shooter and learned two cartridges had been fired. But there was no way for Drake to know if they'd found a target, or not. He mentioned that just before he came up on the hillside he'd seen sign where two horses had stopped, and a mite beyond that he commented to the effect that it appeared some rider had been chousin' some cows, and then drove off a small bunch, though he didn't follow that trail. Anxious to get up on the hillside, I reckon."

Alice put in, "If Buck Drake had looked behind one of these rocks, he might have found my footprints. My boots being smaller than a man's . . ." She left the sentence unfinished.

Jerry grinned. "If I have to, I'll alibi you, Alice."

Mart Monroe continued, "I waited with Drake and about an hour and a half later, a wagon come out from Topango Wells and got Jacklin's body. Drake said he was going to call for an autopsy, in town, but first he aims to have Doc Handley probe out the bullets that finished Jacklin, to see what can be learned from them, if anything."

Jerry gave a short whistle. "Any of your outfit carry a forty-four Colt?"

Monroe considered, then shook his head. "No, do you?"

Jerry nodded, smiling somewhat wryly. "So it will be laid at my door."

*"Pshaw!"* Monroe frowned. "There must be a heap of hombres around, packin' that caliber hawg-laig, but that don't prove you finished Jacklin."

"No, but I'll be a prime suspect." Jerry smiled. "I guess I'll just have to move a mite faster before a showdown comes."

They talked a few minutes longer, then Monroe said he'd better get back and look after the cows Jerry had delivered. He wheeled his horse and started off. Alice hesitated a moment, doing something with her pony's reins, which seemed to be a bit tangled.

Jerry asked, "Does the clerk in this county, marriage license clerk, issue a pretty engraved license with flowers and cupids on it, or is it just one of those plain ones?"

Alice crimsoned. "Jerry, you're going pretty fast—"

"That's my way—All-of-a-Sudden Knight, they calls me. When I see a beautiful piece of scenery, I don't lose any time staking my claim. And about that house on the tableland we're going to build, how many rooms are you planning to have? Maybe you should draw up some plans—"

"I've already made some sketches—" Then she stopped.

"I'll ride over some night to look at 'em."

"Cowboy, stop this foolishness!"

"Who says it's foolishness—do you?"

"We-ell, no, of course—that is—" She bit her lip.

" 'Course you don't," he chuckled. "Just as soon as we get Flecker and Capron cut down to size, we'll—"

"Jerry, you will be careful, won't you?"

"What do you mean—careful?"

"Not get shot—or—or—"

"Doesn't make any difference, does it?" he asked airily. "You said, yourself, I was just a crazy cowboy."

"Well, I didn't mean it that way."

Before anything more could be said, Mart Monroe, who was some distance ahead, yelled back, "You comin', Alice?"

Alice wheeled her pony and took off in pursuit of her father.

An hour passed, while Jerry sat his pony in the shade of a big outcropping of granite and smoked a Durham cigarette. Before long, Wing, Hackett and Reed came riding back. They drew rein at Jerry's side.

Jerry said, "I figured you'd take longer."

Reed shook his head. "We swung the herd near the Two-M ranch buildin's and picked up a couple of their hands to take our places. Met Monroe and his daughter on our way back. Nice folks. Monroe said much obliged for the help we'd given his boys. They got a *muy elegante* spread over there."

Wing asked, "What was done about Jacklin's body?"

Jerry related what Monroe had told him. When he had concluded, Hackett looked concerned. "Jerry, if they probe out those forty-four slugs, it could put the deadwood on you."

"Maybe so." Jerry nodded. "I'm not doing any fretting. C'mon, we'll amble back to the Circle-F, and listen to Flecker blow up when we haven't any word of finding Jacklin."

# XIV

Jerry and the other three returned to the Circle-F just as Cornpone Jones was lugging food up from the cookhouse. Cornpone was a trifle tipsy as usual.

"Hurry up, you hombres," he said, "get them broncs unsaddled and give me a hand with this chow. Lucky, I cooked enough for you—"

"Be with you in a jiffy, Cornpone," Jerry said. Once they had the ponies in the corral, the men gave Cornpone some assistance. Jerry was the first to enter the bunkhouse, where he found George Corwin sitting, scowling, at the long table, impatiently awaiting his dinner.

Corwin looked up at Jerry's entrance. "Where in hell you fellers been?" he demanded in some irritation.

Jerry said, surprised, "You hombres back already? Where's Tim Beadle and Kelt?"

"I'm back," Corwin said shortly. "Jinglebob and Pistol-foot had some fellers waitin' to take over, after we crossed the line. Tim's gone with 'em to take care of things. I come back, case Kelt needed me. He was gone when I got here. But I asked you, where you hombres been all day?"

"Out looking for Jacklin," Jerry said mildly. "We left early this morning, on Kelt's orders."

"And you been loafin' all day, I reckon," Corwin said nastily. "Where'd you ride?"

Jerry grinned provokingly. "Oh, just riding around. You know how cowboys are, Corwin."

"Cut it," Corwin snapped. "I asked a serious question. I want an answer."

Jerry said coolly, "Just how bad do you want it, Corwin?"

Corwin started to swear, then cooled down suddenly, as Wing, Hackett, Reed and Cornpone entered with the food. "C'mon, eat," he growled. "We'll talk about this later."

Cornpone left and the men settled to their supper. Jerry asked once, "Where's Kelt?"

"He had to go to Topango Wells on business," Corwin grunted.

The rest of the meal was eaten in silence. Once finished, the men drifted outside, all except Corwin. Jerry remained near the door, waiting for Corwin to emerge, which he did after a few minutes.

"I want you to understand one thing, Knight," he said angrily. "When Kelt's away, I'm in charge here."

"That's not the way I get it," Jerry said coldly. "Kelt sent us out on a job and he said plain I was in charge."

"That's when I'm not here," Corwin stated hotly.

"Kelt didn't give me any word regarding

you"—Jerry spoke insolently—"and until he does, I'll do things my way."

"Seems to me you're gettin' right cocky, Knight." Corwin's eyes blazed. "We'll see what Kelt has to say about this when he gets back."

"I just gave you information you wanted," Jerry snapped. "When Kelt says I'm in charge, I'm in charge. We've been taking care of Randall Company business and—"

"To hell with the Randall Company and you too!" Corwin lost his temper. "Kelt'll strip your skin off when he gets back."

"For that matter," Jerry blazed, "to hell with Kelt and you, too, Corwin!"

Corwin's eyes bulged, his jaw dropped. "Why, you—" One hand started to descend toward his gun.

"Go on, jerk it," Jerry challenged. "I asked you a spell back how bad you wanted it."

Corwin's face flamed, then he paled, seeing the other men watching him. "Not now, not now," he muttered half to himself. "We'll let Kelt settle this when he gets back. I can see you four hombres have come to some sort of understandin'. I don't aim to be ganged up on. When Kelt returns—"

"Hell," Jerry taunted, "is that all you can say—Kelt, Kelt, Kelt? You say you're in charge. What do you have to wait for him for? Lack the guts to act for yourself? You don't even know what Kelt went to town for, I'll bet."

Corwin struggled to master his temper. "I can't be expected to know. Kelt was gone when I rode in. Nobody here but Cornpone. Cornpone didn't know what it was all about. All's he knew was that a rider had come with a message from Deputy Drake. Drake wanted to see Kelt right off. That's all Cornpone heard. And here you four galoots say you been lookin' for Jacklin all day."

Jerry laughed. "You know something, Corwin? I'll bet Jacklin got into some trouble and Buck Drake is taking care of things."

Corwin's eyes narrowed. "You talk almighty certain, Knight, as if you knew something I don't know."

"That's a big laugh, too," Jerry taunted. "I'd be a heap surprised if I didn't know more than a lunkhead like you."

For a moment, Corwin could only stand and stare. "You're askin' for trouble, Knight," he blurted uncertainly.

Jerry shook his head. "Not asking—making it. I wanted to see if you had any guts."

For a moment Corwin appeared to be taken by an attack of apoplexy. He could only sputter, gasp and swear in frustration. It reached a point where he could stand it no longer.

"B'God and b'Jesus!" he swore. "This can't wait for Kelt to get back. I'm ridin' to town to tell him what's happened. We'll see how fast he puts you back behind bars, Knight—if you live that long."

He wheeled and reentered the bunkhouse and in a few moments came out bearing his saddle, then started toward the corral.

Jerry started to follow him. Shorty Wing caught his arm. "Why not let be, Jerry?" Wing advised. "You've won this round. He's heap bad medicine with a six-shooter. I expected him to draw—"

Jerry said shortly, "I never did like takin' medicine."

Reed said, "Maybe we'd better drift along with you and stop—"

Jerry jerked out, "You fellers stay here. This is my job."

Jerry started down toward the corral. As he passed the cook shanty he saw Cornpone, attracted by the loud voices, standing in the doorway. The other three punchers saw Jerry overtake Corwin halfway to the corral. Hearing steps behind him, Corwin turned back to Jerry and set his saddle on the earth.

Jerry said quietly, "Where you figure to go, Corwin?"

"Topango Wells, like I said. We'll see what Kelt—" He broke off. "Hell, it's none of your business, but we're goin' to settle damn soon who's boss here."

"You're going to stay here," Jerry said flatly.

"So long as Kelt said I was in charge, I'm roddin' this outfit."

"To hell with you!" Corwin fumed.

"That can work two ways, Corwin. If you're not careful, you'll be hittin' the same trail Jacklin took."

Corwin backed a few paces, eyes narrowing. "What do you know about Jacklin?"

Jerry laughed coldly. "I know he won't ever come back here. I met him over on Two-M range and we shot it out. That plain? His body's been taken to Topango Wells. Maybe you'd like a dose of the same."

Corwin stiffened. "You ain't man enough to give it to me."

And a third time, Jerry asked, "How bad do you want it, Corwin?"

Still Corwin hesitated, torn between the desire to reach Kelt with Jerry's confession and at the same time put Knight out of business.

Jerry went on in the same provocative tones, "Here's something else, Corwin. I know who the third man in the Wolcott killing was."

Corwin's eyes appeared about to bulge from his head, the tip of his tongue licked at lips suddenly gone parched. His right arm commenced slowly to bend at the elbow.

"Is that so?" he managed in ugly tones. "I suppose you've told Buck Drake some wild tale—"

"I've never even seen Buck Drake." There was an Arctic-like chill in Jerry's voice now. "But I'm sure planning to. You big enough to stop me—?"

A bull-like bellow of rage was ripped from Corwin's lips. His right arm stabbed down. His six-shooter flashed up in a swift arc that ended in a lance of crimson flame and smoke that was almost blotted out by the thundering detonation of Jerry's forty-four.

A second bullet from Jerry's gun was ripping into Corwin's body even before he struck the earth. For a few moments his booted toes drummed convulsively on the ground, then he lay quite still, a dark stain starting to seep and spread slowly on his woollen shirt.

Jerry looked down a moment at his fallen foe. "That's two for Dennis Wolcott," he murmured. Powder smoke drifted slowly on the breeze.

Running steps at his rear caused Jerry to look around. Reed, Wing and Hackett were arriving on the run, Cornpone Jones just behind them.

Shorty Wing gasped, "Lord, that was fast. You hit, Jerry?"

Jerry said grimly, "He didn't miss by much. I heard the whine of the slug—I think—as it went past my right ear."

Reed said solemnly, "I don't see how he could miss at that distance—and he drew first."

"He drew first, all right." Hackett nodded. "We all saw that."

They stood looking down at the body.

Cornpone said gravely, "Now there'll be hell to pay when Kelt gets back."

Jerry said quietly, "Probably—but I reckon I'll have enough hot pitch to pay the bill."

"But what started it?" Reed wanted to know.

Jerry shrugged. "Well, you heard us niffnawin' at each other before. One thing led to another—you know how things go. We both said things the other couldn't take. When he went for his gun—well, there was nothing else for me to do."

Reed said curiously, "Jerry, we heard him yell something about putting you back behind bars."

Jerry laughed shortly. "That's some sort of illusion he got from Flecker. Let's just say he didn't live long enough to do anything like that."

They looked curiously at Jerry but didn't pursue the subject further.

"There's going to be hell to pay when Flecker returns from town," Shorty Wing said.

Jerry gave a short laugh, though there was nothing humorous in the sound. "That's what Corwin kept telling me," he said.

The sun was well below the western horizon by this time and twilight was swiftly settling in.

# XV

Cornpone was snoring in his bunk, the others seated at the long bunkhouse table beneath the light of an oil lamp suspended from the ceiling, talking in monosyllables. No one seemed to have much to say. There seemed to be an unspoken agreement to await Kelt Flecker's return. There'd be certain decisions reached, but what direction such decisions would take was uncertain.

As Jerry had said, "We'll let Flecker play his cards first, then you hombres can take your cue from what I say."

It was nearly ten-thirty before they heard Flecker's horse. The animal hadn't been coming fast. It was as though Flecker had been doing a lot of thinking on his way. They heard the horse pass the bunkhouse and then head down toward the corral.

Shorty Wing said, "Sounds like he's got something on his mind. Usually, he'd yell for one of us to come unsaddle for him."

No one commented on that.

Flecker's step sounded at the doorway. He looked somewhat haggard and drawn as he entered.

"Back, eh, Kelt?" Jerry said brightly.

"Anybody's fool could see that," Flecker growled.

"Well, I'm not anybody's fool," Jerry said. "Heard you had to go to town on business. Must have been right important to keep you this late. Bristol Capron making trouble?"

Flecker spat, "Capron had nothin' to do with it."

"I see," Jerry said casually. Then, "I hate to disappoint you, Kelt, but we didn't find Herb Jacklin—"

The mention of Jacklin's name brought the eruption.

"Goddamn it!" Flecker roared, features working with anger. "I know that."

"My mistake," Jerry commenced. "Naturally, you'd know, if you didn't see Herb when you come in. I should have—"

"Jacklin's dead!" Flecker exploded. "Buck Drake found the body and sent a rider to tell me to come to Topango Wells. There was poor Herb, stretched out at the undertakers—"

"Dead?" Jerry assumed a look of surprise. The other punchers repeated the words, but their manner was unconvincing, which, fortunately, Flecker failed to notice.

Jerry went on: "It sure must have happened sudden. What was it, some incurable disease—or a heart attack—or—"

"Dammit to hell!" Flecker swore. "He was shot! Shot twice. Some bastard must have dry-gulched him. Wasn't no man livin' could face Herb and beat him to the shot."

"Except maybe you, eh, Kelt?" Jerry put in.

"That's understood," Flecker growled, shaking his head.

"So it wasn't a heart attack," Jerry commented. "Well, I've heard of hombres dying from lead poisoning before. Mr. Samuel Colt manufactures some little capsules for such cases. Sometimes they're good when a feller uses 'em; sometimes they're bad when a feller takes 'em. I'm plumb shocked to hear such news." However he didn't look very shocked. "The deputy pick up any suspects?"

Flecker half-snarled, "Not a damn one! There'll be an inquest held tomorrow afternoon, or day after. They wasn't certain. Drake wants to cast around and see if he can get any more information. He had Doc Handley do an autopsy, probe out the slugs. The bad thing is that Jacklin's body was found on Two-M range. In a way, maybe, that's not too bad, though. Drake has half an idea that some Two-M hand was responsible. On the other hand, Drake asked me what Jacklin was doin' on Two-M holdin's."

"What'd you tell him?" Jerry asked.

"Told Drake that I ordered all my hands never to step on Two-M range, told him it was my suspicion that some Two-M hand had dragged the body up in the brush to hide it."

"Smart idea, Kelt," Jerry complimented.

Flecker growled, "Too smart for that bonehead Drake to understand. He just laughed at the idea. Knight, you sure you didn't see Jacklin when you was over that way, day before yesterday?"

"Wouldn't I have mentioned it to you, if I had?" Jerry demanded. "You already asked me that before. Did you send Jacklin over there to spy on me, or something."

"Hell, nothing like that," Flecker said hastily. "I wouldn't do that to a man. I treat my hands square, I do. And now I'm comin' to the crutch of the matter—"

"Crutch? What crutch? Oh you mean, 'crux'—"

"Don't interrupt me," Flecker rasped irritably. "Them slugs that Doc Handley probed outta Jacklin's carcass, appeared to be from a forty-four gun. Anyway, that's what Drake and Handley thought."

Jerry appeared unperturbed. "Couldn't they say for certain they was forty-fours?"

Flecker fell into the trap. "Nah! They was some battered, havin' struck bone when they hit."

"Well, there's no proof it was a forty-four, then," Jerry pointed out, placidly. "By the time a forty-five hits bone, it gets chips knocked off, reducin' the weight. If enough small lead fragments was knocked off, it might bring a forty-five slug down to the weight of a forty-four."

Flecker scowled, trying to figure that one out. Finally he had to admit the truth of the assertion. "Yeah, could be," he conceded grudgingly, still frowning over the matter. "Anyway, I was forced to tell him, when he asked what my hands carried, that you toted a forty-four, Knight."

"To hell you did!" Jerry looked suddenly concerned.

"Well, God A'mighty, Knight, I got to be honest, don't I?" Flecker sounded almost apologetic. "I swear I hated to tell him. Anyway, Drake says for you to come in and see him tomorrow—wants to talk to you, see your gun."

"I'll go, and gladly," Jerry snapped. "I don't like to be under suspicion. I'm more'n willing to talk to the deputy. 'Course, he'll ask a lot of questions, like what was I doing over on Two-M range—things like that. I'll just have to tell him you sent me and why. I don't aim to be a suspect—"

"Now, now, Knight, don't do nothin' hasty—"

Jerry repeated Flecker's words. "I got to be honest, don't I?"

Flecker frowned and scratched his head. Finally he said, "Well, there's such a thing as going too far. You got to be loyal to the Circle-F. You hold off going in to town tomorrow. No use bein' in a hurry. Should Drake come out here, or send somebody to get you, I'll just say I sent you lookin' for strays and you ain't come back yet.

Maybe we can hold off you talkin' to him until after the inquest is held. I don't want one of my hands gettin' into any trouble. I protect my crew, I do." Abruptly, he changed the subject. "Say, didn't Corwin and Tim Beadle get back yet?"

Jerry nodded. "Corwin got in early today, before we got back from lookin' for Jacklin. He said that Beadle would be along later after he'd took care of the papers and so on. Pistol-foot and Jinglebob had some other riders to herd, waiting just over the line—"

Flecker cast a quick glance at Corwin's bunk, saw it was empty, then asked, "Where the devil is George?"

"We put him down in the barn," Jerry replied casually, "wrapped carefully in a blanket."

"In the barn?" Flecker scowled. "Oh, he had one of his fightin' drunks, I suppose. That damn Jinglebob has some of that rotgut likker over there and every so often—"

"Not drunk." Jerry shook his head. "Fightin' mad, though. You see, Kelt, we had a little trouble. Corwin jumped all over us when we rode in, accused us of loafin' all day. He got sort of abusive in his talk, which I couldn't take. I told him you'd sent us and that I was in charge—as you told me. Remember?"

Flecker nodded heavily. "Yeah, but—"

"Corwin claimed he was in charge here when you were away."

"Could be that's correct—" Flecker scowled.

"You just said I was in charge," Jerry pointed out. "Corwin's name wasn't mentioned."

"Still, you shoulda knowed—" Flecker broke off. "What happened?"

"Well, like I say, he was ridin' us. It got worse after supper. There's some things I can't take. He allowed as he was going to ride in and get you and you'd settle my hash. He got his saddle and headed for the corral, with me trying to straighten out things in his mind. But he refused to be straightened. One word led to another. He finally lost his temper and went for his gun. You see, he didn't leave me any choice."

Flecker went white, then red. "You—you shot George?" His voice quavered.

"What do you expect I'd do?" Jerry demanded indignantly. "Would you stand and take it, if somebody drew first on you? 'Course, I plugged him."

Flecker choked over words. Finally, "You mean to say he drew first and you still was able—? Chris' A'mighty! Something damn funny here. Ain't nobody could beat him to a draw that way. How bad's he hit?"

"Too bad to tell you about it. Corwin's finished."

"Dead?" Flecker gasped. He half rose from his chair, then dropped heavily back. "You're lyin', Knight, if you say he had the draw on you, and you could still down him." He turned savagely to the others. "Any of you see the scrap?"

Reed said, "Knight's throwing a straight rope. Corwin drew first." Flecker shot penetrating glances toward the others who all backed up Reed's assertion.

Flecker looked as though he thought they were lying. "There's somethin' damn funny 'bout this business," he stated furiously. "You fellers are in cahoots with Knight. I figure you're all lyin'."

Steve Hackett said coldly, "We're talkin' straight, Kelt. Hell! Ask Cornpone. He's one of your hands. He saw the whole business."

"Dammit! I'll do just that," Flecker raged.

He stumbled up from his chair, crossed the room to the bunks, and seizing the sleeping Cornpone by the collar, yanked him bodily from the bunk, shaking him viciously meanwhile to get him awake.

"Wha—wha—what?" the cook stammered, stupid with whisky and sleep. "Wha's idea, Kelt?"

"Come awake, goddammit," Flecker swore. "Cornpone, did you see the fight 'tween Knight and Corwin?"

"Could—couldn't miss it," Cornpone stuttered. "They come right past my door, makin' mean *habla* to each other. Sudden, I see Corwin reach for his hawg-laig. Then Knight drew his weapon. I expected to see Knight dropped, but, instead, it was Corwin who hit the ground. Don't know how Knight ever done it—"

Flecker swore some more, turned Cornpone around and gave him a kick in the rear. "It's got so I can't trust nobody," he sputtered angrily. "Go get me a pot of coffee, Cornpone. I gotta think."

Obediently, Cornpone started for the doorway, then paused, "You want some chow, too, Kelt?"

"No, I don't want none of your garbage. I ate in town. Now my stummick wouldn't take nothin'. It's all upset like. Musta been some spoiled food at the Chinaman's place." He resumed his seat at the table, and sat glowering at the others. Finally he began questioning them again, but found nothing he could take exception to.

Cornpone arrived with a pot of coffee, in time, with cups for the others. They rolled cigarettes, waiting for Flecker to renew the warfare, but the big foreman seemed drained, stunned, for the moment. Flecker rose once and from some place in his "office" got and opened a bottle of whisky. He drank several large gulps from the bottle, but didn't offer to pass it around. It was plain he was shaken by the news of the deaths of Jacklin and Corwin.

Jerry said brightly, at last, "I just had an idea, Kelt. When I ride in to the deputy-sheriff, I can tell him about Corwin, too."

"The more fool you," Flecker grated out. "That'd bring on another autopsy, and what do you think would happen when they found your forty-four slugs? It would tie you up to Jacklin's murder. Knight, I want you should stay away from Drake. I've been thinkin' things over. Come mornin' we'll bury Corwin right here. We ain't goin' to say a thing about your fracas."

Jerry said dryly, "That's dang decent of you, Kelt."

"Ain't I told you I always look out for my crew?" Flecker growled. "We ain't going to say a thing. Hush everythin' up. That Drake's a smart hombre. Once he starts questioning you, no tellin' what you might say. All that sorta thing could lead to complications. I want you all to understand, and keep your mouths shut. Anybody don't do that, will have to answer to me."

There was little more said that night. The men finally rolled into their bunks, all except Flecker, who sat moodily staring at the table and now and then taking a drink from the bottle.

That night, Jerry kept his six-shooter handy under his blanket. No telling what sort of an idea Flecker might get after he thought things over.

Sometime after midnight, Tim Beadle came pounding in, and a few minutes later entered the bunkhouse. "You still up, Kelt?" he commented in some surprise.

"I got reason to be up. Can't sleep," Flecker growled. "Get the money?"

"Half, as usual; the rest when the cows has

been sold." He plunked a canvas bag down on the table and dropped into a chair at Flecker's side. "Somethin' go wrong?"

"Plenty," in a sour grunt. "Let's check that cash, first."

Jerry lay in his bunk, listening, and pretending to sleep. He heard the two men checking off tally sheets and counting bills and coins, then Flecker, dividing the money in four piles, "There's yours and mine and Capron's—"

"Hey, you got Herb's and George's in one pile. Didn't Jacklin get back?" He glanced at the bunks. "Where's Corwin?"

"You and me are splitting their money," Flecker said heavily. "Where they're gone, they won't need it."

"What you tryin' to say? Have they run out on us?"

"They're both dead."

"What!" Beadle bellowed. His chair creaked as though he had leaped to his feet.

"Sit down, Tim," Flecker rasped. "Some bastard dry-gulched Jacklin, I figure. Then, this evenin', Corwin had an argument with Knight. Knight killed him—now, sit down, I tell you. It was Corwin what drawed first, accordin' to the rest . . ."

Jerry didn't hear all that was said next. There was considerable violent profanity to spice certain shocked exclamations, then Beadle's furious tones, "By God, I'm goin' to knock off Knight, right now. He can't get away with killin' no pard of mine—"

"Sit down, goddammit," Flecker swore, and there was a sound as though he had jerked Beadle back in his seat. "You listen to me. Take care of Knight some other time, if you like. But right now I don't want no more shootin' round here. We're in a jam if Buck Drake starts snoopin' into things on the Circle-F."

Beadle quieted down while Flecker related such details as he had. Eventually the men quieted and a short time later, Jerry heard them turn into their bunks. Only then did he go to sleep himself.

# XVI

The following morning, Beadle, assisted by Wing and Hackett, dug a grave and buried the blanket-wrapped body of George Corwin on a low hill where a heavy growth of brush covered such disturbance of earth as someone might notice. Jerry wasn't asked to assist in the burial.

He had gone to Flecker after breakfast and asked for his orders for the day. "You'd best just lay low for a spell, Knight. Stick around here, but if you see any riders approachin', you keep hid. It might be Drake or somebody he sends in to get you. I figure we'll all take a rest and 'wait developments. And you keep out of Tim Beadle's way, too. He's plumb riled that you shot Corwin. I don't want no more quarrels picked. You hear me?"

"I hear you." Jerry nodded.

"See that you obey orders," Flecker said gruffly. "We've got enough trouble, as it is."

Apparently, there were no orders for anyone else, either. Flecker sat in his office, sulking moodily. Dinnertime came. The men ate in silence. Once or twice Jerry glanced up and saw Beadle glowering at him, but pretended not to notice.

In the afternoon, Frank Reed spent some time

cleaning his forty-five six-shooter. Shorty Wing and Hackett tried to interest themselves in a two-handed game of cards, but that amusement quickly palled, and they turned to the business of cutting a long circular strip from a cowhide with which to make a lariat. Jerry watched them for a time, then wandered on. As he passed the cookhouse he heard Beadle talking to Cornpone, and slowed step to listen.

". . . an' I'm a tellin' you, it's just that way it happened," the old cook was saying in crusty tones.

"I can't believe it," Beadle snapped. "Are you meanin' to tell me George went for his gun first, and then—*right* then—Knight beat him to the shot?"

"Exactly what I say," Cornpone insisted doggedly. "Go ask them other hands, if you don't believe me."

"Buffalo chips!" Beadle swore nastily. "You musta been drunker'n a hoot-owl. Knight couldn't be that fast."

Cornpone cackled. "Why don't you go ask Knight yourownself, then, Tim? He might answer in a way you won't like." Beadle cursed some more. When he stopped a moment, Cornpone interjected, "An' now, less'n you figger to stay and gimme a hand with these dinner dishes, I'm requestin' polite that you get out o' my kitchen domains. I could use some help washin' up them plates and such. Grab a towel an' make yourself useful for once."

Beadle swore at the old cook. Cornpone broke in with: "Then get to hell outta my kitchen, less you crave this kettle o' scaldin' water in your ugly mug. Go on now, scat!"

And Beadle "scatted." He lost no time leaving Cornpone's cookhouse. He came lurching out of the building, cursing furiously, his features working with emotion. It didn't help matters any, when he spied Jerry standing a few feet away.

"What in hell you doin'—eavesdroppin'?" he snarled.

Jerry gave a short smile. "Well, I couldn't help overhearing a certain lunkhead trying to bully a better man, and not able to get it through his thick skull that Corwin really did go for his gun first. Hope it's all clear to you now."

With an effort, Beadle controlled his raging impulse to draw his gun and even the score. "Gettin' right cocky, ain't you, Knight?"

"Call it that if you like," Jerry stated calmly. "Take my advice and you'll cool down before you get any fool ideas about squaring things for your pal. That was Corwin's trouble—he was too mad to shoot straight."

"Think you're right fast with a six-gun, don't you?" Beadle rasped.

Jerry shrugged carelessly. "Fast enough, I

reckon. Would you like to learn just how fast, Beadle?"

There was the challenge. Beadle tensed. Jerry watched narrowly. No telling what could have happened next, had not Kelt Flecker, at that moment, stepped from the bunkhouse door and, instantly, sized up the situation. A look of anger contorted his face as he bellowed, "Tim! You come away outta that. I warned you!"

Beadle relaxed, then turned toward Flecker and started for the bunkhouse, muttering, as he left, "I'll get you some other time, Knight."

Jerry's laugh taunted him. "You mean you'll try! I doubt you got enough nerve."

Beadle didn't reply as he hastened away. At the door of the bunkhouse, Flecker snarled something at him, and he pushed past and went inside, then Flecker bawled out, "Knight, c'mere!"

Jerry sauntered carelessly toward the bunkhouse doorway, where the furious Flecker awaited him.

"Knight, didn't I tell you I didn't want no more trouble here?" Flecker raved.

"You sure did," Jerry agreed. "I—"

"Yet, the minute my back is turned you and Tim starts collisionin'. What's got into you—?"

"Now, hold up a second, Kelt. I didn't start it. I was just standing there, and Beadle come out of cookie's place and jumped me. I hadn't said a word to him. What in the devil you expect me to do—just stand there and take it? Trouble is, Beadle's on the prod and he can't hold that fool tongue of his. If you ask me, he's flirtin' with a bruise—if not worse. If you hadn't interfered I'd like as not slugged him."

"You didn't start it?"

"Dammit, I'm tellin' you, Kelt. If you don't tell him to lay off me, the Circle-F isn't going to be big enough to hold both of us—and I don't aim to be the one leaving—feet first!"

"Now you hush that war talk, Knight! I'll speak to Tim and tell him to steer clear of you. You do the same with him. You got to take into consideration that Tim is hit hard by Corwin's killin'. He ain't himself—"

"And he won't be himself much longer, if he doesn't learn to keep his nasty trap shut. And you can take that warning to him, too, Kelt—"

"Now, now, don't do nothin' hasty, boy," Flecker said hurriedly. "I'll tell Tim to leave you alone."

"You do as you please," Jerry said shortly. "Just get it through your head, Kelt, I don't like to be pushed around."

Flecker's wrath rose again. "Maybe before we get things settled round here, you'll get pushed plenty and learn to like it too, Knight. I've had just about enough of your cocky ways. And—"

Jerry's insolent laugh, as he strode away, cut Flecker's words short. He glared after Knight, as

Jerry strolled down toward the saddlers' corral. "Don't know what's got into that hombre, last day or so," he muttered. "He acts like he'd been eatin' raw meat." He drew a long sigh. "Well, we'll see who's boss, before long. A word to Buck Drake and we'll settle Mister Jerry Knight's hash, once and for all."

The rest of the day passed peacefully enough. About three o'clock in the afternoon a rider from the ranch in the next county, on his way to Topango Wells, stopped to get a drink of water and water his horse. Flecker engaged him in conversation, asking about conditions in his neck of the range and so on. Before the man had left, he'd dropped a bit of information inadvertently that gave Flecker new food for thought, bringing scowls to his face and curses to his lips, though he said nothing to the others about it until suppertime.

The crew was nearly through supper when Flecker spoke in nasty tones. "That Bar-Forty cowhand that stopped here, this afternoon," he began, "dropped some information I don't nowise relish."

The crew paused in rolling cigarettes and drained coffee cups, faces turned toward Flecker.

Flecker went on. "Now, me, I always trusted Mart Monroe, figgered him as a square upright honest sort of hombre—"

"Isn't he?" Jerry broke in.

Flecker shook his head. "Behind that honest front he puts on, he's a downright crook, if that Bar-Forty hand was talkin' straight. He says as he crossed the Two-M holdin's today, he saw some of Monroe's hands drivin' a big bunch of Circle-F cows to their far holdin's. Now where would Monroe get Circle-F critters if he hadn't stole 'em?"

Jerry said innocently, "Surprisin', ain't it? Can you imagine that? Cow-thieves on this range! I'll be damned! I never thought I'd see such condition—"

"Cut out the funny talk, Knight," Flecker growled heavily·

"Could be," Jerry suggested, "that Monroe is just getting even with you, Kelt. Remember we picked up a couple of hundred head of his—"

"Will you shut up!" Flecker thundered hotly. "You talk too much, Knight. I want to know if you know anything about this?"

Jerry sighed in exasperation. "First you tell me to shut up, then you start asking questions that require answers. Why should I know anything about it? I'd say the best course is, to go to Topango Wells and lay all this before Deputy Drake. You ride to the Two-M with such information and you might start a range war. Suppose I ride in tonight and lay the story before Drake? Put it on his shoulders. You already say you don't want any more trouble around here. I'll ride right now, if you say so, Kelt."

"I don't say so," Flecker bellowed. "Seems to me you're a'mighty anxious to get in and see the deputy-sheriff. What you got up your sleeve?"

"Nothing but my elbow," Jerry answered meekly.

"You keep up your smart-alecky ways," Flecker stated ominously, "and said elbow might have to do some fast bendin', reachin' for your hawg-laig—"

Beadle put in eagerly, "I could take care of that, Kelt—"

"Tim!" Flecker snapped. "I warned you. Now you shut up!"

Beadle fell silent. Jerry said, "See, Kelt, I didn't say a thing to him, and—"

"You shut up, too!" Flecker roared. He went on, in a grumbling tone, "Don't know what gets into some people. A man can't get to think, no more."

The table fell silent. Beadle sat glowering at Jerry. Jerry returned the look with an amused smile that he knew would irritate Beadle. The coffeepot went around the table again. Condensed milk was stirred in cups. Suddenly, Jerry gave a sort of half-laugh.

Flecker slammed down his coffee cup with some violence, splashing the hot liquid over his trousers. That brought on more cursing, ending in, "You goddamn redhead, what's so funny to you?"

"Me?" Jerry queried innocently. "What you talking about? I didn't say anything."

"We-ell," Flecker said somewhat lamely, "you sort of snickered."

"Oh, that," Jerry explained. "I just happened to think of a mistake you made, Kelt."

"Mistake? A mistake I made? I don't make no mistakes," Flecker stated shortly. "What you referrin' to, Knight?"

"You remember that newspaper clipping you had about a stage bandit, you was sure was me?"

"I remember," Flecker snarled, "if you're goin' to bring it into the open. You got your nerve to spill that."

Jerry shook his head. "That's your mistake, Kelt. It wasn't me, after all. You didn't read enough newspapers. If you had you'd have seen a later newspaper that told more about that holdup. You see, they captured that bandit, three days later, and he confessed—"

"What!" Flecker seemed stunned, then, "It wasn't my mistake, after all. It was the newspaper was to blame. It didn't give all the news." He glanced defiantly around. No one said anything. He added in ugly tones, "Did that same paper say anything about a hombre that broke his parole, Knight?"

Jerry didn't reply to that but finished his coffee. The meal was concluded in silence and one by one the men sauntered outside. A short distance from the bunkhouse, Shorty Wing said in concerned tones, "Jerry, I hope you realize you're sittin' on a keg of gunpowder with a burnin' fuse attached. Don't spur Flecker too far. He could be a pretty ugly customer when riled."

Jerry laughed shortly. "And you figure I'm a right careless salesman for said customer. Don't worry, Shorty. I'll sell him my bill of goods yet. I know what I'm doing, but from now on I've got to speed up my methods, before more hell breaks loose. Do me a favor, will you?"

"Certain sure. What is it?"

"Sneak down to the corral and take my saddle. Then fork it on my black, and hide the hoss in that thick brush back of the corral. Flecker and Beadle are still in the bunkhouse. I'll go back and try to keep them occupied."

Steve Hackett asked curiously, "You aimin' to light out?"

"Tonight, if I get the chance. Don't worry. I don't aim to leave you hombres in the lurch. I got business in town. I'll see you later."

Frank Reed nodded. "Don't fret none about us. We'll help Shorty with your hoss and saddle, if necessary. Leastwise, we can keep a weather-eye open. The pony will be there when you want it."

"Thanks, fellows."

Jerry drifted back to the bunkhouse, where he engaged Flecker in desultory conversation. Beadle sat scowling nearby, not saying a word, but with anger building within him every second. Finally, as though he could stand being in the room no longer, he rose abruptly and stepped outside.

# XVII

A half hour later, Beadle entered the bunkhouse, looked quickly around, then asked, "Where's Knight?" Flecker was hunched in a chair at his office desk, a scowl of thought crinkling his forehead.

"I dunno," Flecker grunted. "He left here a spell back. Probably with them other cow-nurses. He's been tryin' to convince me I should go in and see Drake, tell him about our cows Monroe has thieved. Imagine that—Monroe of all people. I always figured I could trust him. There's somethin' damn funny goin' on."

"You're right as hell, Kelt. Them cows, like you say. Then Jacklin and Corwin both killed. I've been thinkin that Knight is playin' some game on his own, pullin' the wool over all our eyes."

"I'm beginnin' to get some of them same suspicions, Tim. Don't feel like I can trust Knight no longer. What I don't like, he's too damn eager to go to Topango and tell the sheriff about our cows. Drake would pick his brains, and we'd all be in a mess. Well, I put a stop to that, I can tell you. If he isn't damn careful he'll find himself back behind bars. There ain't no man livin' can double-cross Kelt Flecker and not suffer for it. I put Knight in his place."

"That's what you think, Kelt?" Beadle said scornfully.

Flecker didn't miss the tones. "What you talkin' 'bout?" he demanded roughly.

"Listen, Kelt, when I was out, I saw Shorty Wing and them others takin' Knight's black geldin' into that brush back of the corral—the hoss was all saddled."

"What you hintin' at, Tim?"

"I ain't hintin'. Looks like to me that Knight is figgerin' to sneak off when he gets a chance—like as not ridin' in to see Buck Drake and spill his guts—"

"To hell you say!" Flecker's face clouded up like a thunderstorm, and he violently struck his desk with a clenched fist. "By God, I think you're right, Tim."

"Well, what you aimin' to do about it?"

Flecker thought a moment, then, cruelly, "Do you have to ask me, Tim? I'll say, what are *you* aimin' to do about it?"

"You leavin' it to me?" Beadle asked eagerly.

"Right! This is the move I've been waitin' for. We can settle Mister Redhead's hash tonight, in a way that will put us in the clear."

"What's the plan?"

"You get your bronc and leave here. Ride far enough to see what direction Knight takes. If it looks like he's headin' for town, you stay well ahead and wait until he shows up. When you get the chance, let him have it. You got a gun and you know how to use it. And keep rememberin', George Corwin was a pal. Here's your chance to square that account. Understand what I mean?"

"I get you, Kelt. Knight meets his finish tonight!"

A few minutes later, Beadle went to the corral, saddled up and rode off in a southwesterly direction. After he had crossed the first hill, he swung his pony around and sat in a clump of cottonwoods where he could have a good view of the Circle-F and anyone who might ride away from the ranch.

A short time later, Jerry entered the bunkhouse, rummaged among the blankets in his bunk as though looking for something, then pretended to put something in his pocket and straightened up. Flecker was sitting at his desk, frowning face resting on one hand.

Jerry asked idly, "Where's Beadle heading? I saw him ridin' away a spell back."

Flecker grunted ungraciously, "I don't figger it's none of your business, Knight, but if you want to know, I sent him ridin' to the Two-M, to inquire 'bout our Circle-F cows over there. I don't want to start no trouble, so I thought I'd let Tim break the news that holdin' our cows was no secret to us. Once I hear what Monroe says, then I'll take a hand, and we'll get things settled."

Jerry nodded. "Probably a good idea. No need

jumpin' to hasty conclusions that could make a fuss. I know how hard you work to avoid trouble."

Flecker didn't reply. It seemed to him that Jerry's tones carried a sarcastic note.

Jerry left and at the corral found Shorty Wing and Steve Hackett looking on, while Frank Reed was currycombing his horse. The sun had dropped below the San Lucias long since and darkness wasn't far from settling in.

Shorty Wing said, "Your bronc's waiting for you back in the brush, Jerry, anytime you get ready to take off."

"Thanks, pards. I'll do the same for you sometime."

"Something else, Jerry." Hackett looked worried. "Tim Beadle spotted us hiding the hoss. He maybe suspected something and has told Flecker."

"Like that, eh?" Jerry said.

"And," Shorty Wing put in, "just a short spell ago, Beadle saddled up and rode away. Where do you reckon he's heading?"

"Well," Jerry said, "Flecker claims that he sent Beadle to the Two-M to make inquiries about our two hundred head of cattle over there."

"Do you believe that?" Hackett asked.

"Not none." Jerry smiled. "He wouldn't send Beadle over there this late in the day. But now I think I know where Beadle's headed."

"Where?" Hackett and Wing asked in unison.

Jerry didn't answer that. "Look here, I'd appreciate it if you hombres would go to the bunkhouse, and drop a hint that you're tired of just sitting round, and would like a few hands of poker. I'm figuring Flecker will jump at the chance to gyp you hombres out of a few bucks, with some marked cards he keeps handy. Just don't stay in the game too long if you're losing. Keep your bets low."

"But what—?" Hackett frowned.

Jerry cut in, "I'll make good any losses you have."

"I wasn't thinkin' about that," Hackett said, "but I don't get the idea."

Jerry explained. "I want Flecker kept occupied until I can make a getaway. Don't want to have him see me leave."

Hackett's and Wing's faces cleared. "We'll take care of it, Jerry." Hackett nodded. He raised his voice: "Hey, Frank, quit prettyin' up that crowbait of yours. He ain't going to no hoss show where prizes is awarded."

Reed came over to the corral bars. "What's up?"

They told him. Reed nodded. "I'll be right with you hombres."

Ten minutes later, the men were seated at the bunkhouse table, with Flecker dealing the cards. He didn't ask why Knight wasn't with them. Flecker didn't need to ask: he knew.

# XVIII

It was almost dark when Jerry walked the black gelding away from the Circle-F, swinging wide for a few minutes, then curving back to strike the road to Topango Wells. Here he kicked the pony in the ribs and sent it into an easy lope, the thought running through his mind, "I reckon it was still light enough for Beadle to see me leaving."

Now there was a night breeze lifting, carrying with it the scent of sagebrush. Within a short time a few stars winked into being overhead, and there came a soft light along the eastern horizon. Mostly the road coursed rolling grasslands, with no points of ambush on either side—except one. Having only been over this trail once before, he had taken note of the terrain and fixed various points in his mind, at the time.

Once he drew rein, listening. He thought he detected the faint sound of hoofbeats some distance ahead. He couldn't be sure, though, so he dismounted and placed one ear to the earth. Now the sounds became definite. Jerry remounted and pushed on at a slower pace.

Twenty minutes later he drew to a halt and tethered the pony to a scrubby bit of brush not far from the road. Then, leaving the road, he circled widely, on foot, to the south. Now there were more stars shining down, as Jerry slipped along with all the stealth of an Apache. He was remembering now that five or six miles from the Circle-F a huge tumble of boulders bordered the trail at one side, with a slight sloping of hillside beyond the rock-piles.

Gradually, Jerry's steps carried him up a slow rise of land. For another five minutes he ascended, then turned slightly back toward the road he had left. Sage and cactus and other brush grew here and there. Now, Jerry dropped to hands and knees and crawled along, taking advantage of every bit of growth to hide his movements. Finally, he rose cautiously and peered down a long gradual slope.

A hundred feet below him was the pile of boulders, with beyond, the hoof-chopped trail to Topango Wells. Here lay the suspected ambushing point. Jerry didn't move a muscle. Five minutes passed.

Suddenly, a man coughed, clearing his throat.

From the darkness surrounding the boulders, came an impatient curse. A moment later, a match flared showing Tim Beadle's features, cigarette in mouth. The match was extinguished. A pinpoint of crimson gleamed through the gloom, faded, brightened again.

Beadle was seated on a rock, rifle across his knees, ready to blast the unsuspecting Knight when he rode past. Jerry's features took on grim lines. Drawing his forty-four, he crawled noiselessly closer. It required nearly five minutes to lessen the distance between himself and Beadle, so cautiously did he proceed every inch of the way.

When he again stopped, Beadle wasn't more than ten paces away.

Jerry spoke clearly in the Stygian darkness: "Drop that rifle, Beadle, and drop it almighty pronto!"

Beadle gasped, "Oh, my God!" The rifle went clattering among the rocks. Jerry could hear his heavy breathing, then, "That you, Knight?"

"Correct!"

"But—but what's the idea?" Beadle was glancing nervously back over his shoulder.

"Want me to tell you?"

"I'd sure like to know." Beadle's tones were shaky.

Jerry laughed shortly. "You've been waiting for me to ride past, so you could plug me."

"Chris', Knight. I wouldn't do nothin' like that—"

"Don't lie," Jerry said sternly. "I had a hunch where you were heading when you left. So it was up to me to outsmart you."

"Honest to God, Knight—" The man's words trembled. The cigarette dropped from his lips in a shower of small embers. "Why should I want to kill you?"

"Don't stall! You know the answer to that one."

Beadle didn't reply at once. He sat on the rock, as before, glancing back. Neither could see the other's face, except as a dull blur in the shadows. Jerry was in a crouching position, some paces away, six-shooter in hand. Jerry snapped, "Don't try to tell me you don't know the answer."

"I—I still don't know why you think I'd dry-gulch you."

"Your own idea and Flecker's orders. Maybe you're afraid I know too much."

Jerry's sensitive ears caught a faint rasping of metal against leather. He thought, "He's drawn his gun. It won't be long now—"

There was no time to complete the thought. Beadle had abruptly slid from his rock seat and squirmed behind a big block of granite. The movement had come so quickly, Jerry was almost caught unprepared, as he threw himself flat on the earth, then lifted himself on one hand, poised gun in the other.

A lance of orange flame erupted from Beadle's six-shooter, and then a second shot, accompanied by thunderous explosions.

Jerry didn't make a move, as his eyes strove unsuccessfully to pierce the darkness. A full minute passed, seeming like an hour to the two men. Jerry's supporting arm was growing cramped, but he didn't dare move now. Finally he emitted a groan-like sound.

He caught Beadle's triumphant mutter: "By God, I got him!"

He raised cautiously from behind his rock shelter, but couldn't make out Jerry's form in the darkness. In his frantic haste to get behind the rock, his sense of direction had momentarily gone awry.

Now, he lifted his six-shooter for a chance shot in what he guessed was Jerry's direction. The gun crashed loudly in the silence, the bullet passing wide over Jerry's head and to one side.

That momentary gun-flash of light was what Jerry was waiting for. Jerry's forty-four roared once, twice, three times, spaced closely together before he lost Beadle's position. The explosions echoed loudly in the night silence.

Beadle uttered an agonized cry of pain, before he crashed down. His body thrashed about a moment, then there was silence again.

Jerry waited, motionless, alert. After all, two men could bluff as well as one. It wouldn't do to get careless at this point.

After five minutes he rose cautiously to his feet. There was no movement from Beadle's direction. He made his way toward the spot from which Beadle's fire had come, then reached down. His searching hand encountered human flesh, rather dead flesh. It seemed Beadle was already growing cold. Jerry scratched a match.

He saw instantly the small light had been

unnecessary. Methodically he plugged out the empty shells from his gun cylinder and reloaded, saying quietly, "That's three for Dennis Wolcott."

Making his way back to where he had left the black gelding, he got into the saddle, and resumed the journey to Topango Wells. A little farther on he found Beadle's patiently waiting horse. Taking the reins, he led it behind him, moving more rapidly now.

An hour later, he was riding down the main street of the small town, nearly in darkness by this time. There were but few lights from buildings at this hour. The restaurant of the Chinese was still open, as was the Mexican chili place. A light shone from the window of Hippodrome Casey's saloon. That was about all. Only a few ponies were tethered at hitch-racks, here and there. There was no one in sight on the sidewalks,

Jerry went first to the building where Bristol Capron held forth as resident manager of the Randall Land & Cattle Company. It was all dark. Apparently, Capron had gone to bed, or he may have dropped into Hippo's saloon for a nightcap.

"That's something I'll check on first," Jerry told himself. Leaving Beadle's horse at Capron's hitch-rail, he rode the black gelding back to Hippo's place, climbed down from the saddle and entered, little realizing a certain surprise awaited him there.

# XIX

A tall, gray-haired man in city clothing stood at the far end of the Topango Saloon bar, talking to Deputy-Sheriff Buck Drake. Drake was a stockily-built individual of about forty, with a tenacious bulldog jaw and iron-gray hair that had a tendency to curl at the back of his shirt collar. He had heavy eyebrows, keen blue eyes and a sweeping "horse-tail" moustache. He was in corduroys and wore his badge of office pinned to an open vest. At his right hip hung a scarred leather holster, carrying a short-barreled six-shooter.

So far as saloon evenings go, the night was still young. A few customers ranged along the bar, with drinks before them, sent cigar and cigarette smoke curling upward to the oil lamps suspended above the bar. There was loud conversation, punctuated with laughter every now and then. Tiny drops of perspiration shone brightly on Hippo's round good-natured features as he worked to satisfy customer demands.

That good-natured look was swiftly erased from his features as he glanced up and saw Jerry just entering, to be replaced by a look of extreme concern. He gestured violently for Jerry to leave at once. Not understanding, Jerry approached the nearest end of the bar for an explanation. No one else appeared to have noticed his entrance.

Hippo looked worried. He set out a bottle of beer and placed it before Jerry, meanwhile making futile gestures toward the deputy and the tall gray-haired man at the far end of the bar.

Hippodrome leaned across the bar, as Jerry took a sip of the beer. "That's Deputy Buck Drake," he whispered, "and the feller with him is named Naughton—Neil Naughton. Naughton come here and inquired about a feller named Jerry Knight. I swore I'd never heard of anyone with such a moniker."

"You old liar." Jerry gave a short laugh.

"All right, you dang idiot," Hippo whispered. "It ain't no laughin' matter. I heard Naughton tell Buck Drake he was on the parole board of the Texas State Penitentiary. Them two's been talkin' mighty serious, but I couldn't listen in on much what was said. If this don't mean anythin' to you, forget I said anythin'."

Jerry huddled close to the bar, the other customers hiding him from Drake and Naughton. "If you mean," Jerry said, low-voiced, "do I want to see Naughton right now, I definitely do not. And I'd just as soon he didn't see me. Last time I saw him we had a sort of an argument. I'll be slipping out in a minute, Hippo. I just dropped in to see was Bristol Capron here."

"He was in about an hour ago, but left. Said

he was headed for bed. You been down to the Randall Company office? He lives upstairs, you know."

"It was all dark, so—"

"Then he's like as not turned in."

"That explains it. I'll drop in later, maybe, Hippo—"

"You get out of here fast, Jerry," Hippo advised earnestly. "Naughton might see you."

"Did Naughton see Capron, do you know?"

Hippo shook his head. "Capron had left when Naughton got here. Naughton just got in, himself, shortly after. The T.N. & A.S. freight caboose give him a ride to Topango. Now, you get out of here."

Jerry was already taking his departure. Hippo looked relieved and turned to catch Naughton and Buck Drake looking after Jerry's departing back. The saloon door closed, again.

Naughton and Drake moved down the bar. Naughton said in crisp tones, "Barkeep, that man who just left—?"

"Who?" Hippo stalled.

"That man who just left. Who is he?"

Hippo shrugged fat shoulders. "You got me. Never saw him before. Just dropped in for a bottle of beer. Some strange cowpoke ridin' through, I reckon."

"You mean you never saw him before?" Naughton pursued sharply.

"Well, er—that is—I dunno. I might have—then again—gosh, I can't remember everybody comes in here—"

"I figure you're lyin', Hippo," Drake stated bluntly. "Now, who was he?"

"Maybe you might call him a friend of mine," Hippo confessed, red-faced. "Ain't seen him in a coon's age—though—just ridin' through—maybe lookin' for a job—"

"Quit stallin', Hippo," Drake said sternly. "What's his name? I know he's a stranger to me, but if you know him, talk! Hell's-bells, man, talk up. What's his name?"

"Name's Pete," Hippo mumbled.

"Pete who?" Drake demanded.

Hippo wasn't a fast thinker. To cover his confusion and stall for more time, he commenced to clear a couple of empty beer bottles from the bar. The deputy repeated his question in a stern voice.

Hippo mopped at the bar with a wet rag. "Well, some folks call him Pete and some call him Bud—I don't know's he ever had a last name—not so far as I know."

Drake swore under his breath. "All right, Bud who?"

Hippo seized another empty bottle and started to turn. To avoid the deputy's piercing glance he glanced down and his gaze fell on a label on the bottle. Then he had an inspiration.

"Name's Weiser—Bud Weiser," he stated defiantly. “Just remembered. Ain’t seen him in a long time, though.”

“Weiser, eh?” Drake stared dubiously at Hippo. “Damn funny I never saw him around before.”

His gaze still on the bottle, Hippo had another inspiration. “Oh, Bud Weiser, he hops around a lot.”

Naughton was beginning to look a trifle dazed. Drake seized the bottle from Hippo’s fist, glanced at the label. He gave Hippo a long look of disgust. “Sometimes, Hippo, you get too funny for your own good. It don’t set well on an overweight carcass. I don’t think you knew that hombre at all.”

“Tried to tell you that in the first place,” Hippo said earnestly, “but you insisted I give you a name, so I done my best, Buck.”

“Your best can stand improvement,” Drake said. “And you tell your friend, Pete-Bud-Weiser, I want to see him, if he comes in again.”

“I’ll do that, Buck.” Hippo nodded, considerably relieved.

Followed by Naughton, the deputy-sheriff made his way to the street. They glanced both ways along the thoroughfare, but caught no sign of Jerry. Jerry’s black pony was still at the hitch-rack, but that meant nothing to either man. The horse could have belonged to any one of Hippo’s clients.

After a few moments, they gave up and

returned to the saloon, Drake saying, "If I spot him around, Mr. Naughton, I'll nab him for you."

Jerry, meanwhile, had left his pony at the rack, purposely, hurried around to the rear of the saloon. "Yessir," he was saying to himself, as he hurried along the backs of buildings, on foot, "I'll bet Mr. Neil Naughton would like to see me. Like as not he's some concerned about my whereabouts, right now. Ten to one, he told Buck Drake all about me, and it wouldn't surprise me if they headed for the Circle-F, come morning: Could be I'll learn something from Bristol Capron, by then."

He ducked quickly between two buildings and emerged on the street, once more, a few yards away from the building occupied by Bristol Capron and the office of the Randall Land & Cattle Company. The building was still in darkness. Beadle's horse was slumped on three legs at the hitch-rack, where Jerry had left him.

Jerry said, "With a mite of luck, Mr. Capron is due for a rude awakening, plumb pronto."

# XX

Approaching the closed door of the Randall Company office, Jerry lifted a clenched fist and pounded loudly. There were a few minutes' silence, then a window on the second floor rasped open, followed by Capron's irritable tones: "Who's there?"

"It's me—Knight."

"What do you want?" Capron snapped.

"I've got to see you, Capron."

"What about?"

"Do you expect me to yell it right out in the street?"

"Any reason you shouldn't?" Capron demanded. "I've nothing to hide."

Jerry emitted a short scornful laugh. "Your story and Kelt's don't agree, then."

There came a short silence, then Capron lowered his voice. "Did Flecker send you with a message for me?"

Jerry said impatiently, "Good cripes, I'm not going to yell out the whole story, here. I'll just say this, hell's about ready to break loose, and you'd best get set for it."

"I'll be right down," Capron replied in uneasy tones. The window was slammed shut.

Jerry waited. In a short time he heard

steps descending from the upper floor. They approached the door. A bolt was slid back, a key turned in the lock. The door opened a few inches. Jerry started within, only to feel the door refuse to give.

Through the narrow opening the barrel of a revolver was shoved toward his head.

"You stay right there, Knight," Capron grated. "Give me Flecker's message."

"Hell, I'm not going to stand here, talking. I'm coming inside."

More of the gun barrel was shoved through the opening. "You'll get a bullet if you try to force your way in here, Knight. I'll tell the deputy-sheriff you tried to break in and rob me—"

Jerry gave a short laugh, stepped to one side and grasped the gun barrel in his right hand, pointing it skyward. "Now, you damn scoundrel, shoot and be damned. Buck Drake is only a short distance down the street, if you want to bring him on the run."

Capron was cursing hotly, trying to wrest the gun from Jerry's hand, and at the same time endeavoring to hold the door closed against Jerry's weight.

"Let go my gun, Knight," he panted. "What business you got here? I demand to be told at once—"

His voice broke in a hopeless grunt, as Jerry wrested the gun from Capron's grasp, and then shoved open the door. Once inside, Jerry thrust the revolver in the waistband of his trousers, and slammed the door shut at his back.

"We've wasted enough time, Capron," he snapped. "No more of your delaying moves. Get a lamp lighted—"

"I won't do it," Capron exclaimed. "I don't intend to stand here and let you break in like this—"

He thrust out one leg to stop Jerry coming farther. Jerry gave him a solid kick in the shin which brought a howl of pain from the man. "Now, get a lamp lighted," Jerry snapped.

Capron's nerve was broken. "Wait until I tell Flecker about this," he wailed, hopping about on one leg. "This is unlawful—"

"If you don't get a lamp lighted," Jerry threatened menacingly, "I'm aimin' to blast you from hell to breakfast, and there won't be enough left of you for Kelt to recognize."

"But, look here, Knight—" Capron began in wavering tones.

Jerry drew his forty-four from holster. "Capron, I'm going to count to three, and if a lamp isn't lighted by the time I say 'three,' you won't ever need a light again." Jerry drew back his hammer with a sharp click. That convinced Capron.

"Hold it, hold it!" Capron half-shrieked. "I'll light up. Give me time."

His bare feet scurried over the plank floor of

the office, as he searched feverishly for a lamp and a match. Jerry grinned in the darkness, but tried to keep his voice stern, as he urged, "Hurry it up then. This isn't my night to be patient."

A match scratched loudly and a moment later a lamp shed a soft glow over the big office. There was a big flat-topped desk with a chair behind it. Other chairs stood nearby. A filing cabinet was near the desk and against one wall stood a big iron safe, with the heavy door closed.

Capron was white as a bleached sheet, his thin hair tousled over his pasty forehead, his balding pate glistened in the lamplight where beads of nervous perspiration stood out. His thin mouth hung open. He had drawn on trousers over a nightshirt, and his suspenders dangled at his hips. Jerry glanced quickly around the room, then moved toward the front wall to draw the shades at the windows.

Capron watched in a trembling silence. "Look here," he quavered, "you don't need to go to all that trouble. Just tell me what Flecker said, and—"

"Shut your trap!" Jerry snarled viciously. He didn't particularly care for the role he was playing, but to further the ends in view it was necessary that Capron be thoroughly intimidated. "Now, come over here and open this safe."

"I won't do it," Capron stated defiantly.

Jerry repeated his order and gave a cold laugh

that made chills course along Capron's spine. Capron gathered some remnants of his swiftly vanishing nerve. "There ain't enough money to interest you, Knight—"

Jerry tilted his gun, saying softly, "I don't advise that you go stubborn on me, Capron. Open that safe—"

Capron had already started toward the safe. "You'd better get out of here, Knight. I know all about you. When I tell the deputy—"

"Meaning what?"

"Flecker told me about you being paroled. You were in prison."

"For what crime?"

"You killed a man," Capron stated in a shaking voice.

Jerry uttered a short ugly laugh. "Then you should realize that after the first killing, the second always comes easier. So don't get any fool notions, Capron. And I reckon Flecker told you just why he hired me on the Circle-F."

"He never said—"

"Don't lie, Capron! He wanted to frame me as the third man in the Dennis Wolcott killing. You know that damned well."

Capron choked and gazed fearfully at Jerry's cold features. "How—how—?" he stammered.

"Never mind how I learned. You get this safe open."

Capron knelt before the safe, trembling fingers

manipulating the dial. A moment later he rose. The big door was swung wide. "I—I don't like this," Capron protested. "I want to see Flecker or one of the others—"

"You sit down in that chair over there." Jerry's gun barrel indicated a seat near the desk. "One bad move out of you and you'll get what the others got."

"Oh, my God," Capron whispered hoarsely. "You've killed Flecker and—and—"

"Shut up!"

The lighted lamp on the desk revealed the safe's contents. Jerry reached to a cash drawer, removed a stack of bills which, with a wide grin, he stuffed into a pocket.

"Is—is this just a holdup?" Capron choked.

"What do you think?"

Capron fell silent, his uneasy gaze following the cowboy as Jerry procured from the safe a couple of heavy ledgers and a packet of papers. These he spread on the desk, before seating himself. Then he opened the books.

An hour drifted past, lengthened to an hour and a half, while Jerry examined books and documents. Finally, recovering his courage somewhat, Capron ventured, "No use you going through those records. They won't tell you where to find more money. You wouldn't know anything about the Randall Company's business."

"I know more than you think. For instance

you were ordered to quote the railroad a decent price for a right-of-way through Camino Canyon. You lied to the railroad people when you asked, *demanded,* four times that price."

"My God!" Capron's eyes bulged from his head. "Has Flecker told you that too?"

Jerry was quick to grasp that advantage. "You'd be surprised some of the things I've learned. What would you think, for instance, if I told you that the F, in Circle-F, might someday stand for Flecker. And then where would you be, Capron? Think it over."

Capron cursed. "Why that dirty dog, that double-crosser. I'll be ruined if this gets out. Listen, Knight, I'll give you some money—lots of money—and you get out of the country. I'll not say a word to Deputy Drake about breaking your parole. I'll fix it with Flecker—"

"Shut up, you sneaking worm!"

"Is Kelt dead, or isn't he?"

Jerry uttered a cold-blooded laugh. "What do you think?"

Capron groaned, tears formed in his eyes and a sob shook him.

Jerry eyed the man with disgust, decided to bluff some more. "You not only deceived the T.N. & A.S., but you've tried to ruin Mart Monroe, so you could hold up the railroad for a right to go through Palo Verde Pass. Flecker has rustled Two-M cows—"

“Knight, please. I’ll do anything you say. I didn’t think Flecker would ever tell that. He claimed to be my friend—”

“Will you stop that sniveling, or do I have to stop you?”

Capron sat in a trembling silence, while fifteen more minutes passed and Jerry continued to pore over the ledgers. To only a small extent had he found what he searched for. It was time for another bluff. Abruptly, he picked up his six-shooter and swung it toward Capron. Capron stiffened with fear and started to beg.

“I’m through wasting time, Capron,” Jerry stated harshly. “Now I want the other book.”

“What other book?” Capron’s eyes had shifted nervously and Jerry knew his hunch was correct.

Jerry shook his head in exasperation. He said in a tired tone, “Haven’t you learned yet not to stall? Do you expect Flecker to keep mum about everything he knows. Dammit! Get that book!”

Capron came to sudden life, scurried over to a point near one end of the desk and started clawing feverishly at boards in the floor. A board came loose and was lifted out, then a second one, revealing a hidden receptacle just below. Reaching down, Capron produced from beneath the floor a large ledger bound in gray buckram. Staggering to his feet, he dropped the book heavily on the desk and wilted back to his chair.

Fifteen minutes later, Jerry lifted his head from

the book and shot a few sharp questions. Capron, shaken to the very core of his thieving heart now, answered readily and promptly. Jerry continued to peruse the pages, asking questions from time to time.

Finally, he closed the book and looked disgustedly at Capron. "You're pretty low," he said coldly. "You were sent here to look after the Randall Company's interest, and you've been cheating the company almost from the start—"

"It was Flecker started me doing that—"

"Don't lie! You've sold twice the number of cattle you've reported annually and pocketed the difference. You've foreclosed mortgages on ranches and small farms you had no right to foreclose, and then sold the property again and pocketed the money, forging records to suit your own crooked, slimy means. You've cheated poor wretches out of their money by selling land to farmers—land that wasn't fit for farming. You've foreclosed again and again, always reselling in your own name and pocketing the money. You've—"

"Wha—what could I do? Flecker threatened me—"

Jerry coldly eyed the man with a certain loathing. "Your bankbooks are here, showing you've made yourself a pretty wealthy man at the expense of the Randall Company. I'm going to see that restitution will be made as far as possible. You've made the name of Ira Randall a thing to be hated and feared in this country. That's an injustice if there ever was one. That will have to be straightened out when you've made a full confession of your crooked dealing. You've murdered when it suited your convenience—"

"I never killed a man, Knight, so help me, I never—"

"You were in it with Flecker and his crew of sidewinders."

"Flecker forced me to it—"

"Lying won't help you now. I don't doubt Flecker had the nerve for it, but it's your cowardly, dirty mind that planned it all—oh, hell, Capron, I'm sick of talking to anyone as lousy as you. C'mon, I'm taking you to Buck Drake—"

"I'll tell him you broke parole—"

"Tell and be damned to you. Up on your feet, stinker!"

"No, no!" Eyes staring, thin lips slobbering, Capron staggered up from his chair, as Jerry rounded the desk. He threw himself on Jerry, clutching at his arms, fighting to get Jerry's gun, now back in holster. Jerry struggled to throw the man off, but the wretch was fighting like a cornered rat with a sort of maniacal strength, kicking, scratching and issuing a certain madman-like gibberish.

"Damn it," Jerry panted, striving to shove the man back. "Quit it. You can't—"

And then the door opened quite suddenly, closed as quickly. Kelt Flecker’s voice grated menacingly through the room:

“Raise ’em high, Knight. You’re a dead man if you don’t!”

# XXI

In desperate eagerness, Capron released his hold on Jerry and staggered back, a relieved sob issuing from his mouth. Then he cried, "Thank God, you're here, Kelt!" Then his voice rose and he screamed savagely, "Kill him, Kelt! Kill the snooping bastard! Don't let him go! Kill him!" He sank weakly into a chair. "Oh, thank God, you're alive, Kelt. Look, don't waste time. Kill Knight now. He knows everything—"

"If you don't hush that yelling," Flecker snapped, "you'll bring the whole town down on us." Capron subsided, tears of joy coursing down his cheeks.

Jerry, hands in air, moved slowly around to catch the triumphant look on Flecker's evil features. Even then, Flecker's finger was trembling on his gun-trigger as though he could scarcely control the impulse to fire.

"God, what luck!" he exclaimed ominously. "I come in to talk to Buck Drake about you, Knight. When I seen Tim Beadle's hoss out front, I wondered what Tim was up to. Then I heard Capron screamin' like a crazy hombre. So I come in and—say, where in hell is Beadle?"

Jerry smiled thinly. He stood with hands clasped across the crown of his sombrero, alert for any opportunity that might arise to get out of this unforeseen predicament. "Hell, Flecker," he said coldly. "Last time I saw Beadle, he was stretched out cold, at a spot where he was waiting to ambush me. Right now, I'd bet on it that he's down in hell, explaining to Corwin and Jacklin how it happened."

"Damn you!" Flecker snarled. "I'll square that, too—"

"Kill him, Kelt, kill him!" Capron squealed frantically. "We don't dare let him live. Use your gun, quick!"

"Shut up, you fool," Flecker spat. "A shot would just bring Buck Drake here on the run. Capron, you get that gun outta his holster. Then we'll truss him up tight, while I try to make him see reason. Mebbe we can make a bargain with Knight. He can probably use money. Remember, the law wants him. Hurry up and get his gun."

Cautiously, Capron approached Jerry from the rear, lifted the six-shooter from Jerry's holster. In his excitement, Capron overlooked his own gun, sticking in the waistband of Jerry's trousers. During the struggle with Capron, the weapon had slipped down considerably. Capron stood between Flecker and the light, and Flecker had failed to notice the gun.

"Speed it up now," Flecker was urging hotly. "Go fetch a rope."

Capron slid Jerry's forty-four to the far side of the desk.

Jerry knew there'd be no bargaining once he was tied tightly. Probably, Flecker planned to use a knife to finish him, thus not risking the noise of a gunshot.

Abruptly, Jerry jumped to one side, reaching for the gun in his trousers' waistband. Too late to prevent the movement, Flecker realized tardily what Jerry was doing.

Flecker's gun tilted in a savage arc, even as he cursed Capron's stupidity. The gun thundered loudly, even as Jerry leaped halfway across the room. Then he had Capron's gun free of his waistband.

A second time the gun in Flecker's fist spat flame and powder smoke. Something red-hot drilled into Jerry's right side, staggering him. He lifted Capron's gun, pulled trigger once . . . twice.

The weapon was of smaller caliber than a forty-four and of cheap construction. The first shot missed. The second bored in high in Flecker's shoulder. With a yelp of pain the big man swerved to one side, dropping his gun.

With a desperate eagerness Capron swooped down and got Flecker's forty-five, swung it toward Jerry. Jerry laughed grimly through the fog of swirling gunsmoke, lifted Capron's gun and hurled it full in the face of its owner, spoiling Capron's aim, but not before a shot exploded from the barrel.

The gun whipped savagely against Capron's

beak-like nose and he sat violently down on the floor, blood spurting from his nose. Jerry leaped to the desk, secured his own gun, just as Flecker stooped to get the gun from Capron's hand.

"Drop it, Flecker!" Jerry yelled. "You're a goner if you don't."

With a curse of rage, Flecker dropped the forty-five, and leaned back against the wall, beads of sweat dotting his forehead, left arm dangling weakly at his side. Capron was climbing to his feet now, half sobbing with pain and fear, blood running down his face from a broken nose.

"Capron," Jerry ordered tersely, "get over there against the wall with Flecker. On your way, kick his gun down this way."

Reluctantly, Capron obeyed and stood, quaking, at the side of his partner-in-crime. Jerry stooped and picked up Flecker's weapon. Now that he had the situation well in hand, Jerry commenced to feel rather weak and relaxed. The wound from Flecker's gun didn't seem particularly painful; he judged it to be little more than a scratch. Seating himself on top of the desk, he laughed grimly.

"Your crooked game is up, scuts."

Flecker swore a vile oath and took a step toward Jerry. He stopped, when Jerry tilted his forty-four. "Come on and try," Jerry invited in chill accents, "if you've got the nerve."

The lifted gun in Jerry's grasp destroyed any idea that Flecker may have harbored about further resistance. “Look here, Knight,” he said, “I mentioned a bargain. Maybe we can—”

The sound of running footsteps in the street interrupted the words. The door was pushed violently back and Deputy Drake entered, followed by the man named Naughton. At their heels were a number of curious citizens, drawn by the gun explosions. They stood crowded about the doorway, eyes wide.

“What in hell is all this shootin’ about?” Buck Drake roared, taking in the situation at a glance, then added, with a touch of humor, “The shootin’s over, appears like.” With that, he shooed the crowd of curious citizens away from the doorway and slammed the door in their faces.

The man named Naughton was eyeing Jerry curiously. “So it’s your doing, eh, Jerry?”

Jerry grinned and said, “Well, I reckon I had a hand in it, Mr. Naughton.”

“You ready to go back to Texas with me?”

“I’m not sure if I’m ready, but if you insist, I might consent to go back for a spell, until things get straightened out—”

Buck Drake interrupted. “Who’s the redhead, Naughton?”

“This is that idiot, Jerry Knight, I was telling you about. He never knows when he’s well off.” His voice took on a bitter tone. “Jerry, I thought you’d get into trouble, but you wouldn’t listen to my advice. Looks as though you almost got yourself killed. How would I feel if I had to return to Texas without you—?"

The door opened suddenly and Mart Monroe, followed by Alice stepped inside. Buck Drake said, "Howdy, Mart, what you doin' here?"

"Well," Monroe confessed, rather heavily, "I maybe didn't give you a straight steer, Buck, when you was investigatin' Jacklin's killin'. It's sort of been on my conscience ever since. I knowed who killed Jacklin, and I figgered I'd best come clean with you."

"That so?" Drake scowled. "That ain't like you, Mart."

"I know it, Buck, and I'm plumb ashamed o' myself, but there was circumstances—well, this Jerry Knight feller run off two hundred head of Circle-F cows and turned 'em over to me, to take the place of a coupla hundred head Flecker had stole from me—"

"That's a lie," Flecker objected. "It was Knight stole them cows. I give him hell—look, Buck, I been hit. I want to get to Doc Handley's place—"

"You'll get there in time," Drake said shortly. "You ain't goin' to die right off. Now, hush up a minute till I get the straight of this crazy business."

"Jerry gave me a bill of sale for the cows he delivered, said that would cover me, if any difficulty arose, and I figgered I'd best tell you about that too—and then Alice insisted on comin' with me, and—” Monroe floundered rather helplessly. “I reckon that’s all. I just wanted to make things straight all around.”

“Knight’s a crook, that’s what he is,” Capron charged shrilly. “Take him in charge, Deputy Drake. He’s a paroled murderer. He broke his parole and took off—”

“Hush up your caterwaulin’, Capron,” Drake growled.

“Capron speaks truth,” Flecker charged. “Just soon as I can get my wound tended to, I aim to swear out a warrant, chargin’ him with stealing Circle-F cows—”

“He took money from my safe too,” Capron whined. “Forced me at the point of a gun—”

“I’ll gag you if you don’t hush up,” Drake snapped. Capron quieted down.

Naughton and Drake exchanged smiles. Naughton said, “Mr. Monroe, let me see that bill of sale Jerry Knight gave you.”

Monroe produced the paper, passed it to Naughton. Naughton examined it, handed it back with, “That’s in order. Jerry had a right to sign that—”

“What!” Flecker cried indignantly. “Sign for the Randall Company?”

“You dang lunkhead,” Drake growled. “*He* is the Randall Company. Owns it lock, stock and barrel.”

“All right,” Jerry said resignedly, “you would

spill it. I figured to keep mum on that until I could get things well cleared up here." A sudden silence had descended on the room. Monroe, Alice, Flecker and Capron were staring at Jerry in openmouthed amazement. Flecker seemed to wilt back against the wall.

"You maintainin' that Knight owns the Randall outfit," Flecker sputtered. Capron gave a horrified gasp and slid to the floor in a half-faint, his legs no longer able to bear him up under the shock.

"Owns all of it," Drake snapped. "He's your boss, Flecker, but I reckon you won't be workin' for him much longer."

"Jerry, you should have told me," Alice cried.

"Had other things to say first," Jerry smiled. "Remember?" He went on, telling in swift detail what he had discovered in the hidden ledger, and of the duplicity of Capron and Kelt Flecker. While he talked, Alice came and sat at his side on the desk. The others listened intently while Jerry revealed what he had learned.

"All this makes no difference," Flecker said doggedly. "Owner or not, Knight is still a criminal under the law. He killed a man and broke his parole—"

"It was Wolcott broke that parole," Naughton cut in.

"Let's skip that," Jerry suggested. "I've got all the dope on Capron and Flecker I needed, even to the identity of the third man in the Wolcott killing."

Flecker went ashen pale. "It—it wasn't nobody from the Circle-F done that killin'—"

"Liar!" Jerry said sternly.

"Look here, Jerry," Naughton put in. "I know Mr. Monroe and his daughter would like to know a bit more about this, about you and—"

"All right." Jerry nodded. "Perhaps it is best that we clear up a few things now." He moved closer to Alice's side, taking her hand in his. She didn't try to withdraw it.

Monroe said, "But who did kill Wolcott, Jerry?"

Jerry spoke slowly, in a rather relaxed manner. "I'm laying that killing at Flecker's door. He had a wallet on which Wolcott's name had been stamped in gold, but Flecker scratched out the letters, much as he could, but not enough. I could still read Wolcott's name, when I looked close. Flecker insisted on me carrying it, figuring that Jacklin would kill me, and when the wallet was found, I'd be accused of the murder." He finished in a rather tired voice: "Oh, cripes, Mr. Naughton, you tell what happened. I'm sort of weary."

"I never gave him no wallet—" Flecker protested.

"If you don't keep your mouth shut, Flecker," Buck Drake threatened, "I'm goin' to bend my gun barrel across your noggin."

Flecker fell silent. Naughton had started to

explain: ". . . and you see, Ira Randall is Jerry's uncle. Jerry could have had a good job with the Randall Company, but he refused—wanted to make his own way and learn the cattle business on his own. He took up land in Texas, near Santone, and built up his outfit. Such independence made Ira Randall angry. He thought Jerry was acting foolishly."

Naughton paused to marshal his thoughts, then continued, "Later, Ira Randall was taken ill. He'd had a bad heart for years. He turned the management of the Circle-F over to a man he thought he could trust—Bristol Capron."

Capron by this time had regained his senses and was just scrambling up from the floor. Now, he moaned, mumbling something about Flecker leading him astray. No one paid the man any attention.

Naughton went on, "Well, we all know now what a crook and a cheat Capron is, though he claims Flecker led him into crime—I figure they're a pair. Meanwhile, a friend of Jerry's, named Dennis Wolcott, had some trouble in a small town in Texas. I understand Wolcott shot in self-defense, but the man who was killed had friends on the jury and Wolcott was sent to prison under the name of Jerry Knight—"

"How could that happen?" Mart Monroe scowled.

Naughton explained. "Wolcott was a stranger

in the town where the killing took place. When arrested, he refused to give his name, but when searched the authorities found a Barlow knife with a silver plate on the handle, and the plate was engraved with the name, *Jerry Knight.* Jerry had loaned the knife to Wolcott one time, and as Wolcott admired the knife, Jerry told him to keep it. The reason Wolcott wouldn't give his name was that he had a sick mother in the East, who would probably have died of shock had she learned her son was a murderer. So Dennis kept still and went to trial under the name of Jerry Knight.

"As soon as he was able, Wolcott managed to let Jerry know what had happened. Jerry said if anyone could be saved worry and pain through the use of his name, it was all right with him. So Wolcott went to prison under the name of Knight and was paroled under the same name."

"Well, I'll be danged!" Buck Drake exclaimed.

"Ira Randall was finally compelled to leave Kansas City and go to Texas for his health. He and Jerry patched up their differences and Ira grew to love Jerry like a son. Randall appointed me his lawyer and it was through him I met Jerry. Ira wanted me to come out here and manage the Randall properties, as he was beginning to distrust the Capron financial statements, after we'd discussed the affairs of the company. I couldn't leave my own business interests right then. I also held a position on the State Board of Paroles, and there were many cases to be settled.

"Meanwhile, Jerry was working to get Wolcott paroled. I arranged matters. Jerry gave Dennis a job on his own ranch, then later, Ira Randall, who also knew Dennis, sent him out here to look secretly into the affairs of the Circle-F. From all I've been able to learn and putting two and two together and surmising a bit, it's my idea that Wolcott caught a man named Ridge Conway stealing cattle. He wrote Jerry about that, but said Conway had managed an escape. Wolcott caught him, red-handed, a second time and the two men shot it out, I figure. Flecker must have suspected Wolcott by that time. Perhaps Flecker will tell what happened next."

Flecker growled. "Aw, this is a pipe dream. I ain't got nothin' to tell. It's all lies."

Naughton said coldly, "You'll tell in time, Flecker. Anyway, the next thing we heard was that Dennis Wolcott was found dead, and Deputy-Sheriff Drake was seeking the killer. Wolcott was supposed to report to his parole board periodically. When he didn't show up, it was erroneously announced that he had jumped parole. About that time, Ira Randall had another severe heart attack, and signed all his holdings over to Jerry. Ira hasn't much longer to live, but he'll finish his days in comfort down on Jerry's Texas ranch—"

Flecker broke in. "Ain't you hombres got no heart? I'm wounded. I got to get outta here. I want to get to Doc Handley's."

"If you don't shut your trap," Drake snapped, "you won't need a doctor ever again." Flecker quieted, but his eyes narrowed, and a turmoil of fear was boiling within him.

"After Wolcott's death"—Naughton took up the story—"Jerry insisted on coming here to make an investigation on his own. I thought it too dangerous. In fact, Jerry and I quarreled about the idea, but he came anyway—took off without telling me, though I guessed what he was doing. To cut a long story short, he's accomplished his mission, but I still wonder he didn't get himself killed. I'll leave it to him to explain how he got in with the Flecker gang—"

"He's not goin' to live long enough to explain nothin'!" Flecker yelled.

Back against the wall, his right hand had darted beneath his coat, and emerged holding a short-barreled six-shooter, which he swung to a low arc to cover all the others. "Ain't nobody goin' to stop me now. Beadle's hoss is waitin' outside, and—"

Scarcely changing position, Jerry's arm jerked his forty-four from holster. He fired in time to divert Flecker's first shot, then fired again, the violent concussions shaking dust from the ceiling rafters to mingle with the spreading powder smoke.

Flecker's body stiffened, then he dived forward to land with a heavy crash on the floor.

Jerry sat as before on the desk, swaying slightly. "Like all fools he had to boast first," Jerry was saying thickly. "I knew . . . he packed an underarm gun . . . whenever he wore a coat . . . noticed the bulge . . . more than once . . ."

His words ceased, his head dropped, then he toppled sidewise, his head in Alice's lap. Alice gave a short scream. "He's wounded!" Now she was seeing the spreading stain along his shirt, at one side.

Buck Drake was bending over Flecker. "Still alive," he muttered disgustedly, then hurried across the floor to Jerry. "Cripes!" he exclaimed, "I was certain that underarm gunshot hadn't hit him. This must have happened before."

Alice wailed, "Oh, Jerry, why didn't you tell us before?"

But Jerry Knight was beyond hearing at the moment.

It was late afternoon when Jerry awakened. He looked about, discovered himself in a bed. One side felt stiff and sore. An exploring hand found bandages. There came a sudden movement at the side of the bed. Alice sat looking down on him.

Jerry forced a smile. "Hello, darlin'. Where am I?"

"At Doctor Handley's house. Wait, you're not badly hurt. Just terrible weak from loss of blood. You should have told us—"

"Didn't figure I was bad hit, and wanted to get things settled, while everybody was there to hear. Flecker—?"

She grasped the thought in his mind. "No, you didn't kill him. And he's going to live. They took him to the hospital in the county jail, at the county seat. He'll live to face trial. Both he and Capron have confessed—oh, so many crooked dealings. They spend all their time accusing each other, then more skullduggery comes out."

"So they'll both face trial and both will get the punishment they deserve. Funny, last thing I remember was sitting by you when Flecker pulled that underarm gun, then I—"

"You fainted from loss of blood, almost as soon as you fired."

"Fainted!" scornfully. "Just like a weak old woman. Gosh, what a fool I am."

"Jerry, I told you, you were a fool the first time I saw you—a fool or crazy or something. I was so wrong." Her eyes were moist.

"And now you don't believe it?" Jerry grinned, feeling stronger now. One arm went around Alice and he drew her face down to his.

"Jerry! Stop! Dad or Mr. Naughton might come in."

"Let 'em come in." Jerry smiled happily.

"The sooner all of Topango Wells knows it, the better—"

"Knows what?"

"About that house we're going to build on that pretty tableland near Palo Verde Pass. Lady, don't you realize I got plans for you and me?"

Alice bent down to complete the first plan. . . .

**Center Point Large Print**
600 Brooks Road / PO Box 1
Thorndike, ME 04986-0001 USA

**(207) 568-3717**

**US & Canada:**
**1 800 929-9108**
**www.centerpointlargeprint.com**